into the wreck

BY THE SAME AUTHOR

FICTION

Tennis Lessons
Common Decency

POETRY

ISDAL

into the wreck

Susannah Dickey

BLOOMSBURY CIRCUS
LONDON · OXFORD · NEW YORK · NEW DELHI · SYDNEY

BLOOMSBURY CIRCUS
Bloomsbury Publishing Plc
50 Bedford Square, London, WC1B 3DP, UK
Bloomsbury Publishing Ireland Limited,
29 Earlsfort Terrace, Dublin 2, D02 AY28, Ireland

BLOOMSBURY, BLOOMSBURY CIRCUS and the Circus logo
are trademarks of Bloomsbury Publishing Plc

First published in Great Britain 2026

Copyright © Susannah Dickey, 2026

Susannah Dickey is identified as the author of this work in accordance
with the Copyright, Designs and Patents Act 1988

"Diving into the Wreck", from DIVING INTO THE WRECK: Poems 1971–1972
by Adrienne Rich. Copyright © 1973 by W. W. Norton & Company, Inc.
Used by permission of W. W. Norton & Company, Inc.

The extract from 'Two Lorries' in Seamus Heaney's *The Spirit Level* is published
by Faber and Faber Ltd. Permission is granted by Faber and Faber Ltd.

'The Shipwreck' by W. S. Merwin. Copyright © 1956, W. S. Merwin,
used by permission of The Wylie Agency (UK) Limited.

This is a work of fiction. Names and characters are the product of the author's
imagination and any resemblance to actual persons, living or dead, is entirely coincidental

All rights reserved. No part of this publication may be: i) reproduced or transmitted
in any form, electronic or mechanical, including photocopying, recording or by means
of any information storage or retrieval system without prior permission in writing from
the publishers; or ii) used or reproduced in any way for the training, development or
operation of artificial intelligence (AI) technologies, including generative AI technologies.
The rights holders expressly reserve this publication from the text and data mining
exception as per Article 4(3) of the Digital Single Market Directive (EU) 2019/790

A catalogue record for this book is available from the British Library

ISBN: HB: 978-1-5266-9171-2; TPB: 978-1-5266-9205-4;
EBOOK: 978-1-5266-9208-5

2 4 6 8 10 9 7 5 3 1

Typeset by Six Red Marbles India
Printed and bound in Great Britain by Clays Ltd, Elcograf S.p.A

To find out more about our authors and books, visit www.bloomsbury.com
and sign up for our newsletters
For product-safety-related questions, contact productsafety@bloomsbury.com

According to the National Monuments Service in Ireland, there are nearly 18,000 shipwrecks in Irish territorial waters.

For the majority of these wrecks, their precise location and history remain completely unknown.

Gemma	11
Anna	67
Yvonne	131
Amy	195
Matthew	249

Shipwreck is seldom a singular event but often involved a myriad of subplots and dramas ... The causes of shipwreck might seem to amount to more than one can estimate, but despite all the technical and social progress to date, these have hardly changed at all. Ships still wreck for the same reasons.

— Roy Stokes, *Between the Tides: Shipwrecks of the Irish Coast*

I came to explore the wreck.
The words are purposes.
The words are maps.
I came to see the damage that was done
and the treasures that prevail.'

— Adrienne Rich, 'Diving into the Wreck'

They began to go
To pieces at once under the waves' hammer.

— W. S. Merwin, 'The Shipwreck'

Gemma

Why did she wear the hoodie into the water?

It's a Friday night in mid-May, and her friends are coming to the beach. As is standard, they're late. They were supposed to arrive at half seven, but it's after eight when Gemma gets a WhatsApp from Rebecca, telling her that they've passed The Red Door, the posh restaurant ten minutes down the road. Neither Gemma nor Rebecca has ever been, but Rebecca has designs on getting married there someday, 'Before I'm thirty, obviously.'

When her phone vibrates with the message, Gemma is interspersing pacing the hall with turning her head left and right in the square mirror above the table. Everyone else is out – Mum had insisted they all make plans, that keeping busy was better than wallowing, and so, Matthew is at one of his mate's houses; Anna, the pub; their mum at her biannual hospice trustee fundraiser dinner. Buoy, the ageing spaniel, is asleep on her pillow by the kitchen radiator. The house is mostly in darkness, and fraught with Gemma's imminent departure, which she's distracting herself from by assessing the asymmetry of her face. On the table is the dusty landline and a bulbous yellow lamp, which invites her to compare the different shadows cast by her nose as she twists her neck. Her phone vibrates again, and she considers giving an excuse – her period has come unexpectedly; the washer-dryer is flooded; the fridge is broken. Her father has died. That's right. Again. She inhales deeply. She replies. Coming!

They pull into the car park in five cars: four girls, four boys. Two cars would have been sufficient, and more economical, but this is the new, unavoidable dynamic of the group: the freshly licensed refuse to cede power, so everyone who can drive does. The cars are of different vintages and display greater disparities in wear: Christina has been granted access to her mum's pristine silver Golf; Jason, who's been working behind the counter in the local pharmacist since before it was technically legal, roars his nasty burgundy Subaru around the sharp bend; Conor and Holly were bought old, beaten-up Fords upon passing their tests, and the cars' prior signs of distress have only worsened under their new masters. Finally, there's Tom in his dad's confusing truck, streaked with agriculture. The convoy makes no sense. Gemma descends the steps from the front door to the road with trepidation, rubbing her arms.

They've all come out from Derry – apart from Tom, who has come even further, from the mythical farm in Claudy nobody has been to. Gemma appreciates them making the effort, though she knows they're mostly here for the beach, that if it weren't for the pull of the sea they'd be at Rebecca's, or Holly's, or the Homebase car park. It's only a half-hour drive to Gemma's, but it wouldn't be worth making if she lived inland. She's a relatively recent addition to this social milieu, and she feels her semi-fringe status constantly. There are well-worn dynamics she can't understand, that she can only catch fleeting impressions of; flirtations and resentments and jokes and betrayals, some dating back as far as puberty. Gemma was brought into the group in September, by Rebecca – beautiful, shiny Rebecca, who always has perfume in her school bag. Theirs is an accidental friendship, a consequence of proximity and sparsity: the AS Level French class with only four people in it. Walking in to the first day's bell, Rebecca had immediately claimed Gemma as her own, throwing herself into the chair Gemma had assumed would remain empty. The other two budding Francophiles are Amanda, who has a kind, dachshund face but biting halitosis, and Scott, who is silent. In a low-stakes arena like this, with an ally like Rebecca, Gemma has found herself newly capable of a bawdy kind of confidence — she can be funny and arch and silly, and the po-faced teacher with the neckerchiefs is often telling her to settle down. Gemma loves being told to settle down — it makes her feel like she's exactly what she's supposed to be.

Introduced to the wider group, it's been harder to find a place to plant a flag. The social terrain is already littered with flags, it might not *need* any more flags. She's been trying, though, and every so often she manages to assert herself within a splinter group of the main faction: an idiosyncratic remark; an unexpected, shared predilection; a cautious bout of teasing. Christina had even squealed, 'You're so mean!' at her, in a delighted way, after Gemma had made a show of over-analysing her very earnest and laborious descriptions of her recent trip to Cornwall.

'They have this really lovely community centre, where they put on different food nights every month –'

GEMMA

'Food nights?! Wow! *Food.* You serious? The Cornish are eating *food* these days? That is absolutely mad!'

It was stupid, but that didn't matter. The trick, Gemma is learning, is that stupid is fine, provided you commit with gusto. Within minutes, Christina was doubled over in an only slightly exaggerated performance of hysteria, and Gemma was proud of herself for having accurately gauged that not only is Christina generous with her laughter, she is also a person you can mock without consequence, being, as Christina is, sincere but not tedious, kind but not wet. After this, Christina was established as a safe ally, someone Gemma could count on to vote for her, should a vote ever determine her value to this years-old coalition.

Tonight is a different kind of gathering. It's not like the evenings in Rebecca's or Holly's, where raucous and drunk games of sardines supplant the need for any one person to be entertaining, or like the nights where the bouncers look the other way and permit them entry to Sandino's, where tequila shots and wet, communal cigarettes do most of the work. Tonight, half the contingent will be sober, and all will be expected to strip to their pants and tackle the sea. Gemma, as custodian of the beach, has been forced into the role of host, and she's not sure how to reconcile her home self with the self that needs to prove itself the same as her peers.

She had another group of friends until this year, a group she decided to jettison last summer. It's not that they weren't nice – they were. *So* nice, in fact. Eight nice, lovely girls of poor social standing, and for five years Gemma was delighted to have them. Every morning before school they would congregate around a radiator in the English corridor, pressing their backs to the hot ridges and draping their blazers over their knees. All of them undisclosed but obvious virgins, they'd talk about Doctor Who or Harry Styles; they'd compose elaborate, off-key songs about fictitious detectives; they'd watch videos of puppy spa sessions and make plans to go bowling or ice-skating at the weekend. It was all very safe, and silly, and easy, and the means by which any one girl could become group alpha were clear and tangible: whose mum had let them decorate their room with *Death Note* posters; who had come up with the funniest new pair of nicknames to distinguish Louise Dale from Louise Dougherty; who was going to get their ears pierced that summer. It felt, in many ways, like a gaudily painted waiting-room – a merry place to bide time before anything real happened.

The problems began when Gemma turned sixteen, and started thinking about sex. She's not sure of the exact moment, but one day sex appeared in her mind like a seed lodged in a tooth, and from then on she couldn't ignore it. She wanted to talk about sex, she wanted to have sex. The others weren't there yet, or weren't willing to admit it, so when Gemma tried to introduce subjects of arousal and desire, the nice, lovely girls would only squirm and giggle and reduce it all to some asinine joke. It wasn't a joke to Gemma, though. Sex had started to dominate every instant of her public and private life. How she chose to express herself, style herself, carry herself, was now dictated by indecorous yearnings, because she knew she couldn't afford to think of any space as definitively sexless. Places that had felt joyful and safe before – the McDonald's on the top floor of Foyleside, or the park by the Foyle Street bus station – suddenly became transmuted by the weight of erotic potential. Every journey home was now unavoidably melancholy, made so by her most recent failure to lock eyes with someone who might want her. Roaming the city centre with her pious, squeamish friends, Gemma started to feel such a pronounced longing for random individuals that she sometimes thought she might die from it, and without anyone with whom she could discuss it, she was suddenly her happiest, most dynamic self when she was alone, when she could fantasise.

It wasn't the first time this had happened, Gemma falling out of step with the people around her. When she'd first arrived at secondary school, she'd tried to align herself with the beautiful, confident girls in her year, the ones who'd immediately adopted the shibboleths of teenagers – wearing make-up, kissing rugby players. Compared to them, Gemma was late to familiarise herself with mascara and depilation and foreplay. She was late to grow into her body, and soon the beautiful girls were mocking her skinny, furry legs, her frigidity. Through force of will she'd managed to defect, and for a long time she'd felt confident that this had been a sublime tactical move – she was now safely socially entrenched until the end of school, at which point she'd be able to start fresh at university. For years, she and her sexless band of giggling pariahs had taken pride in being at odds with the shameless and corny lust of their peers (for this was still, ultimately, school: the flirting was blatant and one-note, the relationships were public and short-lived). What Gemma hadn't realised was that these ham-fisted approaches to libido she and her friends were mocking were in fact a necessary rung on the ladder to a more adult desire – she knows now that romantic clumsiness is not a stage that can be bypassed or fast-tracked. Whether you participated now, or later, participation was mandatory.

It was a Thursday morning in March, as she and her former friends huddled by the radiator, that several things dawned on her: one, she needed to get on the ladder; two, her friends would not be joining her; and three, she was, once again, an outlier. The scales of five years ago had now tipped the other way, and all she wanted to talk about was pleasure. This is why Rebecca's arrival had felt like cosmic intervention, a deus ex machina come to rescue her from life as a eunuch. After a few weeks as their new disciple, Gemma realised just how lucky she'd got, because Rebecca and Jane and Holly and Christina were exactly at the stage where she wanted to be, straddling the line between sexual precocity and guilelessness. Gemma wants to flirt – she wants to want and be wanted. On nights out she sometimes manages to lock eyes with someone and secure a graceless, hungry snog, but she wants more. She wants to be touched, properly. She wants to catch up.

* * *

The cars get scattered haphazardly across the gravelly car park, directly over the road from the only house she's ever lived in, which sits in solitude, hovering above the cluster of empty holiday homes, and lodged in the side of Gollan Hill. She meets her friends by the bins, where the uneven shrapnel first gives way to marram grass. It's the final Friday before study leave starts, and spirits are high. Rebecca clambers out of Jason's car in leggings and a crop top, knotted under her bust. She mimes an athletic stretch, then tugs a six-pack of Magners from the boot. She raises it aloft for a second, calls out 'Yeoo!' Gemma watches as the others remove cans and bottles from back seats, and an intrusive question floods her consciousness: if they were all going somewhere else, whose car would she be a passenger in? Who would claim her as more than just Rebecca's sidekick? Before she can ruminate for too long, Christina bounds over. She hands her a bottle of West Coast Cooler and administers a ferocious hug, the bottle resisting the crush of their sternums. Gemma had asked Rebecca to tell the others her news, to save her from having to explain it, and even though a litany of nice messages had come through at various points that week, it is now clear that none of them quite know how to navigate it in person. Holly and Jane give her friendly waves as they slide their feet out of trainers and into flip flops, while the boys start kicking the muddy streaks on Tom's dad's 4x4. Rebecca wanders over and joins in the hug, and she and Christina murmur how sorry they are into Gemma's hair. The hug breaks, and Gemma shakes her head. She has a free pass to be miserable, but she'd promised herself that she would strive to match their energy, partly because she suspects her dolour is less to do with what has happened and more to do with getting naked in front of her friends.

The sun is low-slung by the time they wobble onto the dunes and onto the beach, and maybe that's why they don't immediately notice the entity, almost camouflaged by the black rocks: a twenty-foot-long mass of metal and seam and bolt, rotted and beached. When they do see it, the group halts.

'Holy shit.' Jason, who makes a habit of knowing everything, for once doesn't have the material for narrative authority.

'How long has this been here?' Rebecca turns to Gemma, who can only shake her head in reply. She hasn't been on the beach since the news of her dad's death – over the last few days the atmosphere of soggy unhappiness has turned to actual rain, the accompanying low fog holding the house in a vice.

She breaks from the group and approaches the wreck, which seems to exist outside of the setting sun's glare. She charts a semi-circle around it, then turns on her phone torch and holds it up to the black chasm beyond the fractured opening, where it must have split from the rest of its former body. The meagre beam does little to illuminate the wreck's innards, and though a couple of the boys try to shove one another beyond the threshold, nobody is quite brave enough to venture in. Gemma peers into the space beyond her torch's beam, failing to translate the blackness.

It doesn't take long for the group inspection to turn from excitable to impatient – everyone's keen to get on with the night's main event. They scramble on, charting a course for a point further down the beach. After a moment, Gemma turns her torch off and follows. A shipwreck has nothing on a young body.

After a few drinks and a few rounds of chat, Conor kicks things off by shedding his sweatshirt. The boys are more ready to quit their clothes than the girls, who preen and prevaricate, moaning about full bellies and cellulite. That said, it's not long before Holly's skirt is on the sand. Gemma eyes her short, tan legs. Christina removes her red, fur-lined hoodie, then her t-shirt, revealing a shiny black sports bra. She looks like an advert for the tourist board, or like the approachable but tactless (by virtue of her inability to relate to ugly people) friend in an American drama. Gemma adopts Rebecca's pace, stripping slowly to her underwear. Rebecca has the large, pendulous breasts of a young mother or a Rubens muse, and Jason doesn't even try to disguise his gazing at the Renaissance extremity of her curves, the coruscating dashes of her stretch marks. Her bra is an adult one, a balconette lined with purple lace, anachronistic with her knickers, which are yellow Dunnes bikini briefs, patterned with white flowers. Gemma doesn't know if her admiration for Rebecca's beauty is abstract or lusty. She does know that she wants to be looked at the way Jason is looking at Rebecca – the way that she, also, might be looking at Rebecca. Jason says, 'Nice pants,' in a haughty, mocking tone. Rebecca purrs, 'Fuck off,' in response. Listening to this exchange, Gemma realises that something is already happening between them, even if neither of them knows it.

The clothes are arranged on the cooling sand in the shape of an extra person, like the sorry individual who has to stay behind.

Gemma's underwear set is new, purchased a month prior from Marks & Spencer. The bra is padded to a greater degree than she'd wanted, so before leaving the house she'd loosened its straps to drop the lumps of her breasts further down her torso. She's worried the effect might be strange, like she has teats. The bra is white polyester with navy ribbon around the cups, the knickers a matching navy. She'd thought the colour combination would be flattering against her pale complexion, but in this light her skin is more blueish than creamy – more like a skirting board than condensed milk. She'd wanted to look like a pretty, soft milkmaid, but she's not sure she even knows what pretty, soft milkmaids look like.

'Are milkmaids still a thing?' she asks Rebecca, adjusting and readjusting her teats.

Rebecca laughs. 'God, are you *that* worried about your prospects?'

There's a lengthy debate over who will brave the sea first. Tom and Ian make a show of nudging Christina towards the tide, and everyone laughs; not because it's funny, but because the environment calls for laughter, for a carefree energy built on the cadences of joy. Since turning seventeen, Gemma hasn't been able to stop herself from fixating on the fact of her own mind, and recently most of her sleepless nights have been born of an ineffectual grappling with what it means to be alive, to die, to have consciousness. It's frustrating, she often thinks, that her thinking about having consciousness has to occur within the limits of her consciousness – it's like her mind is a jukebox that can only play descriptions of itself. Now, she tries to think about how her friends might be judging their own positions within this specific context, within this small section of the world. How do any of them know how to be a person? It is this train of thought that prompts her to say that the boys should go first.

'Why's that then?' Ian says, pretending to square up to her. She wonders if she might love him.

'Yeah, G-bag, make your case,' Jason follows up, dragging his eyes from Rebecca's waist. God, maybe she loves him too.

Too many curious eyes now consider her, and she crosses her arms over her abdomen. She has to say something – it doesn't have to be funny, she just has to say *something* – so she announces that the girls' tits make their bodies buoyancy aids, and wouldn't it be better for the boys' self-esteem and machismo if they prove they don't need the girls to stay afloat?

'We're essentially rubber rings, but with more hair,' she finishes. 'Don't you want to swim like grown-ups, without stabilisers?'

There is a protracted pause, but the mood of the night is on her side. Rebecca nudges Gemma with her hip and calls her a wingnut. Christina does that thing where she pretends to be insufficiently clever to understand what has just been said, gawping and laughing and looking around as though in amazement.

'You chat some absolute shite,' Jason says, but it's with the same tone he used to slag off Rebecca's pants, and Gemma beams at the sea. After some posturing the boys set off down the sand, racing one another. The girls rub heat into their bare arms, laughing at the boys' faltering pace when they realise the tide is further out than they thought.

'Right lads, no time like the present,' Holly says, bending her athletic legs up behind her one at a time, pressing the soles of her feet into her cotton boxers. Jane is in a thong and a vest top, her hair in two short, thin plaits. Gemma is worried that she's the only one in matching underwear, that the reason nobody has commented on it is because they think it's weird. Or maybe there's a policy of not commenting on anyone's underwear, so nobody feels conspicuous. She wishes she could see into everyone's minds. She unfolds and folds her arms again.

Holly sets off, the other girls copying her short, confident strides. Gemma hangs back, looking down at her untaut belly, the mottles of her thighs in the dimming light. She appraises the body of clothes on the sand, then picks up Christina's fur-lined hoodie. She puts it on over her bra, wriggling into the lining's soft cilia. She pursues the silhouettes of the others, casting a last glance at the shipwreck, turning to shadow in the growing gloom.

The tide *is* further out than it looked. Gemma can hear the girls laughing up ahead – Jane falls to the sand in a performance of exhaustion, Holly hauls her upright. Gemma wishes she'd kept up with them – the sand is hard and unforgiving on her bare soles, and without an entourage the long walk is largely joyless. By the time she reaches the water's edge, the girls have swum nearly as far out as the boys, who are floating and roiling on and under the sea's disrupted surface. Gemma takes slow steps in, and the water isn't as cold as she'd expected. At knee height, she rolls up the sleeves of the hoodie and reaches below, rubbing the spikes of stubble on her thighs. As the group ventures further, she proceeds at a glacial pace, the water lapping its way up her legs. The smooth waves lick her genitals, and she flinches with pleasure, and soon she is up to her hip bones, bouncing gently on the stimulus. Each curious wave teases her most sensitive parts, and she starts to feel a gentle heat in and around her pelvis. She feels exposed, aroused. As the sea inches up her body, she hoists the hoodie higher and higher, until eventually she is forced to lift it over her head and sling it round her neck, like it's a sheep she's rescued from a forest fire. She regrets putting it on – she wishes she could take to the water undaunted – but she can't go back to shore now. The girls are beckoning her closer, and more conspicuous than the hoodie would be the admission that wearing it was strange and stupid and at odds with everyone else's behaviour. Now, the water is soaking into the padding of her bra, and the new weight of saturated, dense foam coaxes her deeper, until she is in up to her nipples, her arms raised to hold the hoodie clear. The others have decided to have a race, so Rebecca swims along the coast, becoming small and vague in the evening haze – she's the finish line. Ian declares the starting point, and then there is more deliberating about whether people should go on 'three', or on 'go'. Gemma is on her tiptoes on the seabed, occasionally pedalling for the irresistible feeling of silken motion. She has a total ease of body below the surface, at odds with the awkward arrangement above. Rebecca bounces in the distance, holding one arm aloft while paddling in place. Ian bellows the countdown.

As the 'go' arrives, the relative peace of the scene is obliterated. An ecstasy of splash and gasp and tussle thrusts itself north; a frenzied shoal of bodies traversing this small portion of the North Atlantic. Tom grabs Holly's foot and hauls her back, and she responds by whipping her other leg in an arc, her shin making contact with his neck. He slips under the surface then emerges instantly, choking and swearing. Jane has slid up and onto Christina, forcing her to swim as a swan does, with its young on its back. Jason and Conor are jousting, elbowing one another off course while trying to steal ahead.

It feels alien, having this much noise break through the deep coral stillness of the air – from here, Gemma can't even hear the cars passing by on the road. There's only the muffled hum of the breeze and the alto splashes of the tide. Her friends' voices sound metallic, like gongs layered across one another in a harsh and jubilant polyphony. Ian laughs at the chaos he's released, then glances over and sees Gemma, bobbing at a distance.

'What are you doing all the way over there, Gemmo?' he calls.

'Just having a little float,' she calls back.

'Why don't you come over here? We can make bets on who's gonna win.'

She could cry, now, at the conflict she faces – all she wants is what he's offering. She wants to have interactions so throwaway as to signal deep intimacy, and yet, how to explain that she can't come any further because of the hoodie, because she has worn Christina's hoodie into the water and has therefore made herself its custodian. She watches Ian glance back to the action of the race, and though she knows that if she does nothing it will not matter, that the consequences of this missed interaction will be minimal, she nevertheless feels a profound sense of loss. She might not get a chance like this, with him, again.

'Okay!' she calls. 'Coming!'

She balls the hoodie on top of her head and ventures forward, navigating the sand on pointed toes. A sleeve slips past her ear and grazes the top of the sea. She swears. She pauses to fix it, taking a step forward to plant her feet firmly in one spot. Instead, her right foot presses down through the water's gauze to find... nothing. There is nothing, a hole in the seabed – the flat plain gives way, and her body gives way too. Her right leg extends, keeps going, and going; she trips on the unexpected nothingness, she goes down. The lid of the sea closes over her.

* * *

It is thick, dark, numbing. The invisible forces of the vague amnion settle to hold her in place.

She forgets for a moment that her eyes are closed, that the cold water doesn't maintain its own night below the surface. With her lungs half-filled and the heavy log of fabric on her head and neck, her right foot finally meets the floor, and her knees bend to take her closer. She feels something drift away, and she recognises it as her prior conception of being, the notion of her own individual, extant personhood – in the prism of the sea she feels porous, like all life is floating in and through her, like she is floating in and through it. She imagines her erstwhile sense of self crying upwards as it departs, floating up into the space between wet and dry. Her new, shared mind sits in stasis, part of the sea's huge continuity of bodies.

The abstractions of her life assert themselves more clearly, in this moment, as everything silences itself. She remembers that there is a world happening up there, even though that world is incompatible with this, with what she is becoming now. The conditions of that life present themselves to her for idle assessment.

She was shut in her room last Saturday afternoon, watching Britney Spears videos on YouTube, when there was a call from the landing – her mum's voice, asking that she come downstairs. Gemma was supposed to be revising; she's always supposed to be revising. That she rarely is is not part of any grand teen rebellion, just a capitulation to her persistent lethargy. She has aspirations, albeit nebulous ones, and it's not the case that she doesn't want to do well in her exams, because she does, she wants to go to university. The problem is that she is both smart and without purpose. She has figured out a way to do well in exams without any enthusiasm for the subject matter, and without retaining anything of what she learns – all that outlasts the curriculum is the mark she receives, which is always good enough.

Her GCSE results were, for some reason, a disappointment. They were good, better than most people in her year, and probably most of the province. The problem was that they were not perfect, and therefore an affront to the vision for her life that Mum has erected, one she has unwittingly become a participant in – a vision she now realises is a bad joke. Sobbing into her hands as her mum consoled her over her excellent grades was a joke. Her mum insisting on several exam re-marks, and on speaking to the headmaster when he did not invite Gemma to attend his Oxbridge application prep course – that was a joke.

The headmaster beckoning to her in the hallway after assembly and whispering that she was very welcome to come if it meant that much to her, even though, in his opinion, it wasn't the best use of her time, was a joke. Sobbing *again*, in the school toilets this time, was the biggest joke of all.

She did not work especially hard for her GCSEs. Too focussed on sex, she hid her phone inside the cover of her history textbook and scrolled through Instagram, like some caricature of a caricature. She doesn't want to apply to Oxbridge, but the idea that she should, first suggested by her mum and then endorsed by her own fanatical participation – fuelled almost entirely by several rewatches of *The History Boys* – has taken hold. When she fails to get in, that too will be a great disappointment, over which they will once more console each other, as though any of it matters. She's bored of these stupid benchmarks, scattered at random across the landscape of her immediate future – how have such low stakes engendered such melodrama?

Knowing, as she does now, that her academic prospects will likely neither surpass nor fall below a narrow set of satisfactory integers, means that fear, the thing that drove her previously, has waned. When she finally gets to sit her AS Levels (currently postponed, for bereavement purposes), she will likely do fine, as she will likely do fine, also, in her A Levels. She won't go to Oxbridge, but she *will* attend university, where – absolved of needing to get a job by her mum's correlation of affection with financial support – she will almost certainly once again do fine. Her lack of specific ambition means everything feels indistinct, and now that she's lost respect for the sanctity of 'the plan' there is no reason to exert more effort than is necessary. At university, everyone will have similar exam results, but not everyone will be a virgin.

Maybe it would all be different if her reasons for wanting to go to university were different, if the appeal of doing so existed beyond its most superficial associations. Take Rebecca, for instance. Gorgeous and certain Rebecca. Rebecca wants to be a journalist, so Rebecca is going to study History and Politics at Queen's, and then do a master's degree in journalism at the University of Ulster. Rebecca has decided this is preferable to doing an undergraduate degree in journalism, which is offered at some universities, because she wants 'a strong socio-political education to underpin her writing craft'. This is an actual sentence that she came out with, and Gemma could only blink at her, because unlike Rebecca, university for Gemma was not a means by which to achieve some long-held vision of a life, it was simply an arbitrary conclusion to childhood, a space that might foist upon her the clarity needed just to exist in the beyond. She needed to go somewhere that wasn't here, and university seemed as good a place as any. Look at Anna, with her house-share in London and her jokes on Instagram stories about taking her Microgynon with a glass of rosé. Anna is not liquid, taking the shape of any vessel into which she is poured, mutable and irrelevant. Anna knows how to dictate the terms of her world, she knows how to design her life, and surely that only started when she left home. Gemma has to go to university because she doesn't know how else to become real, a person capable of certainty. The subject ranking of the university, relative to other universities, is irrelevant.

Which is why the last few weeks have been largely devoted to Britney Spears videos. She's not sure why it's Britney Spears, specifically – the songs are all ancient – but she knows all the lyrics now, can roughly arrange the visuals in correspondence to the music when she tries to recreate it in her mind. As for standard deviation, she'll figure it out when she needs to.

She was watching 'Circus' when she heard her mum's voice through the door. She watches the videos on her laptop with one earphone in, so she can't be blindsided by intruders. 'Circus' is one of her favourites because of the blatant product placement at the beginning – the smudged, Vaseline-lens shot of two bottles, one the pink diamanté orb of Britney Spears' 'Fantasy' eau de parfum, the other an aqua-blue bottle of 'Curious' eau de parfum, with a thread-bound atomiser. Gemma and Matthew are really into product placement in old music videos, at the moment. Even when they're a room apart they'll send each other links, mocking the pop stars who most brazenly display their corporate sponsorships and brand extensions. Matthew likes Katy Perry's 'Part of Me' because he recently read a succession of tweets detailing how it's just one long recruitment video for the US military. He linked the thread in the group chat they share with Anna, and even she loved it – she doodled a series of cartoons based on the video, each one with a speech bubble in which she'd adapted the lyrics to be about imperialism. Gemma didn't really understand it (who is Lockheed Martin?) but she was so happy that Anna was participating that she replied, Hahahahaha

Britney was just getting into the second verse, where she explains what the two types of men are, when Gemma heard her mum's voice through the door.

She paused the video and removed her earphone, but by the time she'd proceeded to the landing her mum had already managed to get downstairs, where she was waiting by the base of the banister. She told Gemma to come down, and Gemma was half-amused, half-irritated by this stupid game of orienteering, especially when she was pretending to revise. When she got to the hall her mum was in the kitchen, and what Gemma thinks about now is how it took her longer to catch up with her mum's bizarre tour of the house than it took for her mum to tell her that, in the early hours of Wednesday morning, her father had jumped from the Foyle Bridge.

The sea seems to be warming around her. She rubs her arms, and her skin feels like the soft silicon of some strange amphibian. Her breasts are pressed upwards by the padding in her bra and by the water's benevolence. She concentrates her efforts on staying in the small bunker. She digs her toes into the sand and presses her heel into the flinty edges of a rock.

It's strange how well-trodden images or ideas can take on a meaning beyond themselves, how they can stretch beyond the syntactic limits of the words. To someone who wasn't from here, who hadn't heard the way the bridge was spoken about, who hadn't seen the helicopters circling, or had explained to them by their mum at a young age the physics of jumping onto water from such a great height, this sentence might have left some room for ambiguity, or enquiry, or hope. But 'onto' – not into – was the right word here, and for Gemma there was no ambiguity. Her father jumping from the Foyle Bridge meant that her father was dead, just as his having done so in the early hours of Wednesday morning meant it had taken a day or so for his body to be recovered, but even this was a kind of good thing, for some bodies slip away and take weeks to show up, are barely recognisable when they do. Language can carry more, sometimes, than you expect.

In some ways the conversation with her mum, excluding the preliminary game of hide and seek, went exactly the way Gemma might have expected it to. Her mum was gentle, but also prim, and Gemma was silent, trying to massage her thoughts into feeling. She had last seen her father a month ago, as she had seen him the month before that, as she had seen him once a month, almost every month, for the last seven years. She tried to align the mental corpora she had of him with this new information, but they refused to tessellate – the new image, of the bridge with the figure tumbling from it, did not slot in amongst the old images. There was no teleology of the old as they pertained to the new. There was only a new, unquantifiable variable, another side to a man who has always been a mystery.

In the absence of a response, Gemma had watched her mum; a person who also makes little sense to her, but from whom she has at least been able to collect more data. She inspected her mum's expression for signs of pain or shock or anguish, finding only the same slightly irritable preparedness. Her mum was a doctor until recently – an oncologist. She retired, early, at the end of last year, to focus on the hospice, and Gemma has been waiting for dividends. She has a working theory that oncology might be the worst job there is for someone with healthy children, for it seems like Gemma and Matthew's lives have been largely presided over by 'perspective', by the swinging rhetorical scythe of 'there are people dying'. The fact that 'perspective' rarely seems to extend to their mum's own reactions to their domestic transgressions – dirty shoes, wet towels – is just one of the riddles of their family life.

She was around twelve when she realised that her mother's temper scared her. She doesn't know if Matthew has ever felt the same way, they tend to keep the tone of their camaraderie upbeat and flippant: shared looks and rolled eyes and celebrations when they are left alone in the house. If he has the same wariness of their mum, he doesn't say, just as she doesn't. She wonders, though. He's been acting strange recently – even more taciturn and touchy than usual. She wonders if he's thinking wistfully about his departure, the way she is. It might seem a contradiction that her desire to leave doesn't rouse her from passivity, but then the risk of her under-achieving to *such* an extent that she gets trapped seems too small to take seriously. Even Anna, who got shit results, who didn't even do her A Levels, left. Bad results can't stop you leaving, as long as you're bold and determined and selfish, which is what Anna has always been. Gemma desperately wants to be Anna.

In her dent on the shallow seabed, Gemma can feel the vibrations as her friends wrestle and scream – their kicking legs send pulses through the waves, and the surface of the sea shatters repeatedly. She opens her eyes, but can't see anything through the thick fog of blue. She presses her heel harder into the rock.

The aggravating thing about Mum is how excellent she can be when it suits her, so why doesn't she just decide to be excellent all the time? On occasional Sundays she will take them, unprompted, to the chippy, and they will eat battered sausages in the front room with a shitty horror film. Sometimes she envelops Gemma in a hug before she goes to bed, muttering, 'Night, pet,' into her hair. Why, when this is always an option, does she not take it? Surely the unpredictable tension that suffocates the house for days at a time can't be fun for her, either.

Having delivered the news to Gemma, her mum then broached the matter of greater importance: Matthew.
'We need to make sure we tell him in the right way.'

Gemma's initial outrage at this was undercut by her embarrassment at feeling outraged, because shouldn't she have seen this coming? That her mum had told her while Matthew was out running was not because of the news' urgency but part of a carefully curated strategy. It seems at times like their lives are built around shielding Matthew, be it from domestic responsibility, hypothesised anguish, or just anything remotely inconvenient.

'Is there a *right* way to tell him?' Gemma had asked, hoping her scepticism might make her mum realise the ridiculousness of this plan.

'Don't be difficult. You know what I mean.'

When Matthew arrived home, Gemma and Mum were pairing his socks and unpacking the dishwasher. He was allowed to drink his protein shake, dunk his wet shorts into the laundry basket, then dart upstairs to take a lengthy shower. Only after these ablutions were completed was he told in soft tones that this was going to be difficult to hear, but his father was dead.

'Your sisters and I are here for you,' their mum said, stroking his wet hair. He cried, but in a way Gemma thought was a bit performed: all embarrassed red eyes and a diminutive sniff. Gemma was told to boil the kettle.

Matthew is only a year and a bit younger than her, but it's never really felt that way, because at some vital moment she was divested of vulnerability in her mum's imagination in a way that Matthew wasn't. What prompted this allocation of binaries – Matthew soft, Gemma hard; Matthew to be coddled, Gemma to be assigned tasks – Gemma can't fathom, but for some reason she was made the bearer of her mum's worldliness, a fellow sentry at the gates of her brother's naivety. From the moment Anna left, when Gemma was eight, she became the conch into which her mum whispered her confessions, fears, agendas and curses. Her mum has always wielded an all-knowingness over the world, an unwavering ability to perceive, assess and cast judgement. Her intelligence makes her a sort of despotic clairvoyant, for a less clever person would seem like an idiot if they tried to speak so frequently in the language of 'I thought that might be the case' and 'I knew that would happen'. As it is, Gemma feels pretty confident that her mum has never been surprised by anything, not least her ex-husband's death. Not only can her mum foresee the outcomes of others' errors; if placed in the same position, her mum would handle things better.

Because of this, Gemma's appointment to the role of confidante feels like a gift, like a bequeathment from some abstruse deity, because how worthy must she seem to have been granted access? That the role comes with an implicit assumption of Gemma's resilience is also, in some ways, a compliment, because Gemma knows her mum values stoicism in a woman — 'so articulate and dignified,' she used to murmur, every time the mother of the murdered Strangford girl appeared on the news. Maybe this is why Gemma didn't react to the news of her father's death: not because detachment would elevate her in her mother's esteem, but because excess emotion might demote her. With any other kind of person, she would have feigned the sadness she didn't yet feel, but with her mum she knew the right way to react was not to.

The wall of her held breath is starting to wobble in her chest. She can feel the deepening thump of blood in her temples. The hoodie's furry curls waft like anemones at her neck.

She'd asked if there was a note, because she knew from books and films that that was something that happened sometimes. There was a pause, during which her mum looked alarmed. Then she said no, and Gemma understood that this will have been difficult for her – her mum is not someone who sits comfortably with a lack of information. Gemma felt guilty then, because she realised she had asked *not* because a note would make any of this make more sense but because her mum might respect the intelligence of the question, of Gemma's clear-sighted approach to the matter at hand. Gemma nodded, and Matthew said nothing, and after a moment her mum looked more like herself again, and continued in her measured way to deliver details of what would happen next. The only funeral Gemma had ever been to was her grandmother's, when she was one, so she began picturing it: a sombre church affair, with black lace and handshakes. Gemma didn't own many black clothes, so did that mean there would have to be a shopping trip, the acquisition of a grief-appropriate outfit? Anna would be there, and Amy, and they would all perform some ritual of farewell, dressed in their gothic ensembles. Her father would be gone – what did that mean?

She liked her father, though he was a bit strange. He was very nice, but watchful, and quiet. She doesn't remember much from her early years, but after he returned from whatever he was doing in America for half a decade he was a fairly steady presence in their lives, and she didn't mind it. He'd take Matthew and her for dinners, or to the cinema, or for walks along the quay. He'd drive out along Railway Road to pick them up, then drive back to return them. They never stayed at his, because of his new girlfriend, the new girlfriend who was considered an affront to the old wife. Mum was always grumpy on the days Gemma and Matthew were scheduled to see their father, and if it transpired that they'd also seen the new girlfriend, she acted like they'd been duped, lured into the lair of a villain. The thing was, the new girlfriend, Sasha, was perfectly nice too. She came to the dinners sometimes, and she always asked them about school and plans and friends. When they were little, she'd get them selection boxes for Christmas, and as they matured, the gifts did too, into the realm of generous but impersonal – gift cards and book vouchers. He always gave them money, was always asking if they had enough money, as though it were some pressing, urgent concern. He'd also ask them if their mother had enough money, which Gemma never knew how to answer.

He insisted upon telling them that he loved them, at the end of every outing. Gemma always said it back, and she thinks she meant it, though she's not sure how to prove that. Matthew said it less frequently, and always with a certain squirm, which might have just been a boy thing, but Gemma also thinks the sentiment was probably truer of him than her, and it was thoughtfulness that stopped him from reeling it off mindlessly, because for him the stakes were higher. Gemma was happy to say it, regardless of what she might actually have felt, because it felt nice to say it, and because she didn't want to upset her very nice, very generous, very occasional dad.

Does she regret anything? Ought she to have tried to know him better? He was never very forthcoming with personal details – they'd always just talk about Gemma and Matthew's lives, or about films and holidays. On Anna's rare visits home from London, Gemma was always bewildered by how she would enthuse at the prospect of seeing their father, as though an audience with him was some brilliant treat, whereas Gemma couldn't help but think their time with him was mostly a fulfilment of duty on his part — to protect the sanctity of his new life, he needed to be seen to still care about his old one. Maybe for him, seeing his children was low-risk, high-yield, or maybe it was all just a way to atone for leaving in the first place, and maybe that was okay, because maybe most relationships are at least partly transactional. After all, Gemma wonders sometimes if her deference to her mum is primarily motivated by the fear of her mum's eventual death. One day her mum will be gone, and Gemma doesn't want to feel wretched when that happens. There must be worse incentives in life than social duty, right?

It feels like she's been down here forever. What if she has some superhuman ability to hold her breath? The pressure is starting to get uncomfortable, though. Her diaphragm is contracting and expanding in a desperate, fruitless way. The reflex of breathing, without breath. The hoodie is an interesting item, down here – it has a density, yet feels diaphanous. She can feel its mass on her shoulders, yet none of it is real in the weightless antechamber of water.

She will want her mum to feel loved, when she dies, even though she makes it so difficult. Gemma thought retirement would relax her, but it seems that her intensity is fixed, maintained, and replenished by her spirit. Without work, her scrutiny has been newly concentrated upon their home, and Gemma isn't sure the home can bear it. Take the so-named 'family dinner', for example, scheduled for Monday evening, after the funeral. Her mum is approaching it with all the aggression of an army drill sergeant, has been agonising for days about securing the huge, farm-fresh chicken, which as of this afternoon is perspiring in the industrial fridge-freezer in the garage, balanced atop the fancy houmous and the fancy tonic and all the other items she and Matthew are forbidden from snacking on. Why does a dinner require such drama? The problem is her mum is not a woman built for idleness – a blank slate exists to be scored; every day needs an itinerary. Should things not go to plan, the response is always disproportionate, catastrophic – as though a well-planned routine can fix the world's ills, as if a well-roasted chicken can fix a family. Gemma finds herself yearning for the day that she will leave home, for the reprieve it will bring, only to feel immediately loathsome for wanting to leave, because to leave is to leave her mum, to consign her to the bygone days of Gemma's dependence. Gemma will have left to become an adult, and it is during this time that most people's parents die, that her mum will one day die, and there is no itinerary that can prevent it. It's unbearable.

Her father will have died on, or shortly after, impact – that's the physics of it. Even if he didn't die upon touching the water, the resultant concussion will have left him unable to resist the river's flow. The high velocity impact will have transformed the water's surface to a solid, incapable of giving way to a foreign body's volume. He won't have had a moment like she is having now, feeling her heart protest its captivity.

Her chest is now rocking with the force of her lungs' need – her eyes are pressing against their lids. She adjusts her foot against the rock and something sharper than stone bites at her heel. She flinches at the pain, and in one final movement she reaches down to touch her assailant, finding not a stone but something stranger and finer and more delicate. She grips it tightly, then presses onto the ball of her right foot. She sends her body upwards.

She emerges, gasping. The hoodie is drenched, heavier than a spaniel. She rubs her eyes with one hand and blinks blearily into the dusk. She looks around for her friends, prepares her apology: she's sorry for disappearing, for scaring them, for acting so weird when everyone is just trying to have a good time. When her focus returns, she realises she's facing the wrong way – the beach and the wreck beckon from the landscape. She rotates. Ian is where she left him, a small figure embellishing the seam of the ocean. He's not watching, he's laughing. He's facing away from her, towards the still undetermined results of the race. Gemma was only underwater for a minute or so. Water and salt run from her nose and over her chin. She wipes at it dazedly. How long could she have stayed submerged, her absence going unremarked in the world above? How long before someone looked for her? She finds the higher level of seabed, then brings her right hand out of the water. Gripped in her fist is a pair of glasses. Formerly gold-rimmed, maybe; now ruined, and brown, and grubby. One lens is broken, a sharp point poking out of the frame. She imagines a body, lost to water, the glasses cast from their eyes by a forceful current. She emits a squeal, then some strangled combination of a gasp and a sob. Did her father worry that nobody would notice he was gone? Did he feel trapped inside the limits of his own mind, like she does? She can't ask. Maybe if she had before, he wouldn't have thought her so easy to leave behind. He is someone she will never know any better than she did. She drops the glasses, watches them dissolve in the translucent depths. She turns and retreats to shore, tears intermingling with sea.

She'd been distracted before, when they were looking at the shipwreck, but as she arrives back on the beach she watches it, as though someone might leap out. She wraps the hoodie around her legs, trying to dry it with her limited body heat. She opens the bottle of West Coast Cooler and drinks deeply. She waits for the others to return.

She wakes with a headache among damp sheets. The curtains, closed haphazardly, direct a caustic beam of light into her eyes. She groans and wriggles down the mattress, pulling the duvet over her head. With each second comes lucidity, and she's able to reckon with the patches of sediment rubbing at her skin. She hadn't showered when she got in, has brought the beach to bed with her. It exfoliates between her toes and chafes the sensitive skin on her inner thighs. Under the duvet, the environment is humid and dank – the pocket of flat, recycled air smells of sweat and stagnancy. She presses the duvet up and back, closing her eyes against the light. Opening one eye, she squints at the bedside table, looking for her phone. She draws it in and braces herself.

The WhatsApp group has forty-three messages in it: jokes about the contested results of the race; flirty recriminations from the drivers about the sandy footwells of their beloved cars; abashed apologies for things said while drunk; and fifteen photos, taken variously by Holly and Jane, of everyone, huddled together on the dark beach. Christina was the only one with the foresight to bring a towel, and in each of the pictures it is draped around someone's shoulders, until the final few shots where it is laid on the sand, accommodating as many bodies as can be squashed onto it. Gemma zooms in slowly on each face. Most of the photos are awful, but in one she and Rebecca and Ian are curled together on the towel, legs intertwined. Rebecca and she have t-shirts on over their wet bras, but Ian remains shirtless. His thick, rugbied thighs cover most of Gemma's lower torso and hips, and her shins look long and slender, stretched by their placement in the bottom third of the lens. Her face is in three-quarters profile, and there's a dreamy, drunk squint in her eyes. She stares at herself for a while. It's a good picture – they look good together.

She has a separate message from Rebecca: Get in okay, bb? Gemma apologises for not replying last night.

No sweat Rebecca says, instantly. Even if you'd been in grave peril, I was probably too drunk to do much about it. How's the head today? Has Yvonne got you ironing socks yet?

Now that she thinks about it, it's a bit strange that she's been granted this Saturday morning sabbatical from household chores. Maybe this is what happens when someone dies. Gemma feels an intense swell of love for her mum in this moment, then realises that the last stretch of the night is fragmentary and poorly focussed in her memory. She asks Rebecca if she embarrassed herself.

Of course you didn't. Though I think Christina was a bit confused about you taking the hoodie into the sea. A laughing-face emoji keeps it light, but dread floods Gemma's attention.

Is she annoyed do you think?

Of course not!! She said you didn't need to bother washing it but at that point you were a little insistent, so she just let you roll with it. Another emoji, crying with the force of its rictus.

Gemma exhales and tries to soothe herself with repetitions of no big deal and it's fine. She glances around for the evidence. There's no sign of the hoodie on the floor by her bed, where her wet shorts and t-shirt and underwear lie in a dispirited heap. Her desk is littered with open textbooks and half-drawn mind maps. Her wardrobe is open, with her horrible funeral outfit hanging from a bar on the door's inner panel. The make-up mirror has caught the light, and in the punishing glare all the smudges of fingerprints are hyper-vivid. No hoodie though. Shit.

She tries, with renewed vigour, to assemble the night's final moments, curling into a ball as she remembers the 2 a.m. ascension on all fours up to the house, followed by the clumsy scrabble to get her key in the front door. There was teetering in the hall, then a noticing of the droplets raining from the hoodie's wet sleeves onto the wooden floor. There was panic, and then the hoodie was left on the hall radiator, where it has no doubt been found by her mother. Miraculous, really, that this wasn't sufficient to send her careening into Gemma's room at 8 a.m. with a brittle inquisition.

She'd better figure out what her story is – her mother has an inexplicable aversion to lending and borrowing clothes. Assuming responsibility for another person's possessions makes her mother anxious, and anxiety makes her angry.

Was there something else, though? After the hoodie? She glances around the room for assistance, comes up with nothing. She groans into the pillow, feeling her own anxiety mounting. She thinks about messaging Christina to apologise, but when she unlocks her phone there's another message from Rebecca: Seriously don't sweat it about the hoodie. It's just your hangxiety talking. You can give it back to her whenever.

Gemma thanks her for her counsel – she uses that word, 'counsel', in an attempt to formalise and make silly what she knows is excessive gratitude for a small amount of effortless emotional management. Rebecca replies, I'm at your service, my liege and Gemma is reminded of her good fortune – to have someone with this much charisma and sex appeal and social cachet be invested in her well-being. The comfort of it spurs her from bed, and as she pulls clean pants and pyjamas over her sticky, salty body, she listens out for the sounds of the house. The radio blasts a tinny echolalia from the kitchen, and a moment later the hot water tank, hidden in the cupboard next to Gemma's room, squeals into life. Anna must be in the shower, which means Gemma will not even get a stay of proceedings while she has a piss – she'll have to go straight downstairs, where the other toilet is, where the hoodie is, where her mum is.

'Morning, Gem.'

The kitchen, normally a warm cream, is practically ochre in the strengthening morning light. Her mum is wiping the counter, and the usual mound of damp sheets of kitchen roll oozes by the sink. She always has six to seven sheets on the go at once – the vigilance needed to ensure that anything at any moment can be polished or swabbed. If Gemma ever discards one of these sheets, as she sometimes does on reflex, it's not long before her mum is bemoaning the global scourge of Gemma's generation's rampant wastefulness. Gemma has a surreptitious look around for the hoodie, which was missing from the hall radiator. Still no sign.

'Morning,' she says into the bright room.

'Good night?'

'Yeah, it was nice.'

'Bit of a late one?'

'Oh, sorry, did I wake you?'

'No, no. I was awake anyway. I don't sleep until I hear you come in.'

'Oh, whoops.'

'Don't worry, it's just the curse of being a mother.' She accompanies this with a wink, and Gemma laughs, though she is careful to ensure that it's a laugh that relays a genuine appreciation for the sacrifices her mum makes, rather than one that suggests she thinks the joke doesn't have a hard truth behind it. She approaches with caution, and she knows the laugh was deployed correctly because her mum kisses her on top of her head. Her mum is a tall woman, broad-shouldered and athletic and sturdy. She rarely wears pyjamas beyond the threshold of her bedroom, and her outfit for this lazy morning is black skinny jeans and a green t-shirt. She gestures to the kitchen table. 'I left those out for you. I thought you might be in need.'

Gemma wanders delicately to her place. On the place mat is a tube of Berocca, a box of paracetamol, and a box labelled Buccastem.

'Antiemetics,' her mum says, pre-empting the question. With this, another facet of her mum's bewildering complexity makes itself apparent. Gemma inspects the box.

Gemma's experience has never been the same as that of her friends who have strict mothers, nor of her friends who have lenient ones. The justice system at Gollan Hill is perpetually in flux, which is why Gemma never feels able to relax, fully – if earth is not permitted to settle, nothing can ever grow.

She wonders how to navigate this new instance of unexpectedly progressive parenting. Her brain is a hunk of gristle in her skull, denying her the answers. She's usually adept at navigating her mum's moods, is much more skilled at it than either of her siblings. 'Gemma is highly emotionally intelligent,' a school report once offered. 'She is also, however, seemingly reluctant to engage in class.' The obvious connectedness of the two statements did not seem to occur to Mrs Aiken, nor did she seem to give a moment's thought to how Gemma would have to use her emotional intelligence to manage her mum's reaction to being informed her middle child was engaging insufficiently at school. University will be different – she'll no longer have to put a careful spin on third-party perceptions of her social acumen. She'll be left alone, to learn or fail to learn as she sees fit.

The words blur on the box in front of her. She opens it and turns the blister pack over in her hands.

GEMMA

She urges her thoughts to speed up. To take the pills would be to admit that she has overdone it, that she can't be mature with alcohol – this might provoke a lecture about substance abuse, or responsibility. That being said, she really needs the pills: the last time she'd had to conceal the intensity of her hangover from her mum she'd boked twice over her naked body while huddled on the floor of the shower.

She giggles, takes the risk. 'Thanks.' She dissolves the Berocca in water, then uses it to swallow the tablets. Her mum laughs.

'Do you want something to eat? Or are you too fragile?'

'Um, yeah, maybe.' She's not that hungry, but she gets up to retrieve the wholemeal loaf from the bread bin. She waves it. 'Do you want any?'

Another laugh. 'I had breakfast hours ago. Sure, half the day is gone – I've been to Lidl while you were in your pit.'

Gemma squints through her headache. 'But you were there yesterday.'

'I need to keep up with the rate you people eat at. Plus, I realised I'd forgotten a few things to have with the chicken on Monday evening.' She gestures to the rack under the window, freshly piled with potatoes and carrots, a cranial ball of cauliflower. Gemma looks at the veg, once more wondering just how much emotional weight a roast chicken can carry. Something intrusive begins itching at the corner of her memory, then – the familiar chill of the concrete tiles conjures a vision of waddling into the kitchen at 1 a.m., soggy and hungry, kneeing Buoy's inquisitive nose out of the way. Her face breaks suddenly into a yawn, and her mum interrupts her soupy thoughts. 'You can't possibly still be tired.'

Gemma glances at the clock. It's eleven.

'You just don't sleep enough,' she says.

'If I slept any more, nothing in this house would get done. It's not the laundry elves that process that everflowing wash basket, you know.'

The washer-dryer is trundling in the utility room. Gemma swallows a spike of bile.

'I can sort out the things that are in there, if you want, when it's done,' she says.

'What's that? Oh, I don't actually know what's in there. Anna threw a load of stuff on without asking me, and without emptying the basket, so now the dirty towels are just lying in a heap, fermenting.'

Gemma says nothing. She watches the thin filaments of the toaster glow. Her mum continues to rub at invisible stains on the counter.

'I thought we might get a less difficult version of Anna this week, given the circumstances, but that was probably too much to hope for.'

Gemma wills the painkillers to work, to smooth the painful edges in her head so she might navigate this thought experiment. If she agrees too ardently, she risks volunteering as witness for the prosecution the next time a fight breaks out between Mum and Anna – 'It's not just me, you know, Gemma agrees with me that you can be selfish.' Alternatively, she risks a comparative assessment of her own foibles – 'You're very quick to condemn your sister, but there's none of us is perfect.' If she says nothing, though, it might be taken for disagreement, which risks a lengthy performance of lonely martyrdom, a treatise on how Yvonne has never been treated with enough respect by her children, even despite the sacrifices, the sacrifices so numerous and obvious as to not even warrant description. When her mum trots out this monologue, Gemma imagines how she would reply were she more like Anna, fierce and promiscuous with her emotions. She hates how her body immediately responds with the telltale signs of her cowardice – tears threaten her eyes, her voice, safe and cogent inside her head, stalls. No matter how certain she is that there is an answer which, if delivered correctly, will pacify her mum and render her reasonable, she is nonetheless terrified that her endeavours will backfire, that she will only amplify the wrath. As for Anna, she argues with their mother like a mother is dispensable, and not the lodestar upon which their preservation depends. Gemma is either too weak, or too tightly secured in the home's emotional network, to willingly threaten its disruption. Instead, she reserves her anger for the shower – a thousand hypothetical feuds safely abandoned when the dial is turned and the water stops. She's jealous of Anna, but the family's structural integrity couldn't withstand two of her.

She opts for a short, hollow laugh, then a benign murmur. Emboldened by dehydration, she throws her arms around her mum's waist from behind. She mews into her shoulders, 'You're so good to us. Can I make you a cup of tea?'

A palpable fork in the road. A held breath.

'Yeah, go on then, I'd take one. Thanks pet.'

The starched moment softens, settles gently into the current of morning.

The last time she saw her father was in the car, in the family hatchback he seemed to possess purely for transporting Gemma and Matthew. Matthew wasn't there – they'd already dropped him off at a friend's house – so it was just the two of them, making their way to Gollan Hill to the sound of a Saturday afternoon radio quiz. He asked her how she was feeling about her exams, and she said she felt okay. He told her that she would be fine, and this made her grumpy, because how could *he* know that she would be fine. Then he said, 'Don't let your mother put too much pressure on you – no outcome is ever so bad that it can't be fixed,' and she had to look away, because she didn't trust how comforted she felt. When he said, 'I love you,' in the driveway, as he always did, she said, 'Me too,' and the way he hugged her made her into a child again. This is the awful thing, she thinks, about being someone's offspring: no matter how badly she might want to think of herself as an individual, her parents can always tug on the leash that binds her to them. The sensation of that is maybe the opposite of sex, not only for how it manages to completely eclipse, for a moment, her incessant thoughts of sex, but for how it reminds her that her maturing, wanting body will never outgrow the babyish dependence she felt when her father hugged her for the last time.

Much later, when she is shut in her room, she recalls the shipwreck. The rain is falling steadily, engraving the roof over her head. She's scrolling back and forth through the beach photos, trying to decide which one is the best, when she remembers the thick metal artery of the wreck, furred at its edges, lodged next to the rocks. She types into the group chat, Hey, remember the weird boat thing on the beach? but deletes it before sending, not sure it's interesting enough. She muses over whether to tell her mum about it, but the impulse is swiftly dulled by her consideration of the consequences. The day has gone remarkably smoothly, why risk the emotional bureaucracy?

What happened to the hoodie, though? She tries, once more, to assemble the evening's final third – Jane teaching Tom to do a cartwheel, too drunk herself to execute one successfully; Rebecca and Holly bickering in a forgettable way. Then, a third-person perspective on her own body, almost prone on the beach towel, prodding Ian on the thigh and muttering something tearfully in his ear. Oh God, what did she say? She sprawls her arms across the desk and lays her head upon them, groaning. She opens a separate chat with just Ian, types, Hey, sorry if I was chatting shit last night. She deletes it.

Hey, how's the head today? She deletes this too.

GEMMA

Hi she types, hitting send with a fervid flourish. Panic sets in immediately, as she realises she needs to follow it up with something.

At this moment, her aunt's car surfs the road's horizon, sliding into the driveway. For some reason the passenger door is open, but secured to the car's body with green rope. Gemma groans, locking her phone. She curls into a floret on her chair and watches her aunt disembark her stupid sports car. She has a new fringe that the wind wastes no time in mocking – it gets thrown up from her face in a perfect, intact rectangle, like a clothing label stitched to the seam of her hairline. She opens the boot and is beset by fat hold-alls, which collapse into and onto her. One lands on the tarmac and Amy swears audibly. Gemma laughs. She retrieves her phone. The message to Ian is delivered, but unopened.

Amy's here she texts Rebecca.

Oh God

I know

Maybe she'll be more chill than usual, considering what's happened?

I can't be arsed with any of it. I just want to SLEEP

I feel you. Mum wants us to go furniture shopping, and I'm still absolutely hanging. Not convinced I won't throw up on a pouffe

Pretty sure that's a hate crime

Pretty sure you making that joke is MORE of a hate crime

Lol

Good luck with the fam

Good luck with the soft furnishings

Gemma plugs her phone into the charger under her desk. She hears the front door open, followed by the abrasive yelps of her aunt's enthusiasm, followed by the gravelly yelps of Buoy's. Gemma remains on her chair, recomposing her ponytail in the mirror and trying to oust the feeling of dread, the feeling that there's something hiding amidst the lacunae in her memory. She rubs some tinted balm on her lips, then steels herself for the loud evening. As if on cue, her mum's voice vaults up the stairs, 'Gemma, Matthew, Anna – Amy's here.' Gemma slides her feet into her fake Ugg slippers, then opens the bedroom door, nearly tripping over a small mound. She looks down at it. It's the hoodie, neatly folded and clean-looking. Gemma glances around, then takes it into her bedroom. She gives it a cautious sniff – it's been washed, and tumble-dried. She exhales, rubbing her temple to assemble her scattered thoughts. Matthew opens his bedroom door, looking wan and exhausted. They say nothing, exchanging a mutual look of resignation. They go downstairs.

Anna

She's in bed by midnight, but awake until after two, messaging Alex. He's strolling home from a party in Crofton Park, sending her blurry photos of familiar landmarks – the house just shy of Ladywell High Street, where they once found an abandoned copy of a Michel Faber novel; the French café where they often go for breakfast after a big night; the Salvation Army car park where the foxes congregate to scream and fuck. She's not quite sure why he's doing this, but she loves that he's invested these innocuous spaces with lore. The messages that accompany the abstract snapshots vary from irrelevant to confessional. Probably nobody else would be able to infer drunkenness from them, but she can – a missing word, a misspelt adverb, a certain mawkish silliness; all are a deviation from his usual dry precision. He's drunk, drunker than she is, for once. She knows she should tell him that she's going to sleep, but she can't. Instead, she keeps her phone on vibrate under her pillow, so that every time it shakes she is ousted from rest and back to the blue-lit glare of irregular chat. Her hope is that, if he doesn't take the initiative and say goodnight soon, she will fall asleep, and that will conclude things. If she falls asleep while waiting for him to reply, then she's blameless – she hasn't cut the conversation short deliberately, and therefore she won't have actively denied herself the possibility of him saying something sweet or significant. She will also have provided herself with an excuse to message him in the morning, to apologise for having fallen asleep. An additional, albeit unlikely, bonus might be that he'll feel so rueful at her unprecipitated departure that he'll realise a ten-minute lapse between responses is not a satisfying way to communicate with someone, especially after 1 a.m.

Because she is still awake, she hears Gemma attempting to come in. Anna's bedroom is on the ground floor, next to the staircase, so she hears the dispute between Gemma and the lock – the clumsy scraping of the surrounding PVC with her key. It sounds like a dog, scrabbling to gain entry. Eventually there's the

ANNA

atonal clunk of the mechanism, then the door jittering in its frame. A second later, a clatter, as the key, and something else — shoes, maybe — are dropped on the hall floor. Anna is half-tempted to get up to witness the spectacle, never having seen her little sister drunk. But then the phone voot-voots under her ear, so she slides it out and squints at it.

She hasn't been dating Alex long, but the force of her limerence is even greater than she's accustomed to. She's been trying to dilute it, with lengthy bouts of self-rationalising, and occasional shags with other men. The shags weren't her idea; Alex has said repeatedly that they are not exclusive, that they should try and keep their nascent courtship casual. He even has an account on Hinge. He tells her these things with tortured candour, as though it is not a decision he is making but rather an unavoidable hardship they must endure. She doesn't feel much enthusiasm for these other, errant fucks, and she's not actually convinced that Alex is fulfilling the terms of the contract *he* drew up, given that he is always either with her or messaging her. Nevertheless, she'll be damned if she announces her desire for monogamy first.

Alex is recently out of a lengthy relationship, which is how he justifies the need for these codicils. Anna met him at a party in Peckham five months ago, at which point he'd been single for three weeks. It's a recent habit of Anna's, falling for men who are freshly untethered. For a long time, she would date chronically unattached men who treated her terribly. After things came to a head – either in an explicit way, when her poorly concealed yearning drove them to disdain, or in a silent way, when they drifted off without explanation – she would invariably discover that these voluntary bachelors were now in serious relationships. Of the nine men she has dated with intent, four are now married, three are cohabiting, and one remained *so* committed to his singledom that he is now training to become a priest. A man will cut his teeth on your bones before scampering off to gorge himself elsewhere.

The final, unaccounted-for man of the nine is Jack, whose demotion from Anna's attentions was simply an accident of timing – Alex showed up right when things with Jack seemed on the cusp of finally moving forward. Alex's arrival, however, offered her some much-needed clarity: she was now able to see just how much ignominy she'd endured with Jack. His unexpected lean-ins, followed by retreats;

his declarations and qualifications; his apologies, his slights. Jack, like Alex, was recently out of a serious relationship, and Anna soon came to realise that often a self-declared 'decent' man will so doggedly devote himself to honouring the past, that he will merrily shit all over the present. The behaviour of 'good' and 'bad' men can be charted on a horseshoe: polarising motivations meet in the middle, manifesting in near-identical fuckaboutery.

Anna worries sometimes that her changing tastes are not indicative of a maturing spirit, and the only reason she now prefers unwitting criminals to obvious villains is that they pose the greater intellectual challenge, and are therefore a much richer source of cognitive dissonance. It's embarrassing to be in your late twenties and still dating obvious duds, but if you can pivot to the unavailable men who nevertheless have a record of commitment, and that by all accounts *should* be right for you... Well, then you not only have the potential for a high-yield investment, you also have a great fairy tale to obsess over, because maybe *you* are desirable enough to pull off the impossible – maybe *you're* special enough to tip the scales and win him over.

She also worries that her fresh addiction to these kinds of men has less to do with their virtues and more to do with the rationing of their emotions — she is only afforded so much consideration, the rest earmarked for the memory of their former partner. This restricted style of intimacy makes her ravenous, desperate to prove herself worthy of the whole precious cache of a man's interest.

There is nothing Anna wants more than to refute these theories by making it work with Alex. If she can wait it out — if she can woo him through this liminal, post-break-up space into a new era of prosperous coupledom — then she will know that she truly loves him, that she isn't just attracted to her own misery.

It's strange to be messaging him from her childhood bed — she hasn't slept here with any real frequency since she was sixteen. Curled up in flower-print bedding, she can feel time collapsing in on itself, as though everything that has happened between the night she left and now has been compacted into errant matter, which now orbits her duvet. She is both sixteen and twenty-six, an adolescent, virginal ingénue and an adult, worn down with cynicism and bad sex. That said, the romantic hopefulness she can't stop harbouring makes her feel in many ways even more naive than she did when she was a teenager. It's easy to be a doubting realist when you live in a fantasy; it's the dispiriting tedium of practised heterosexuality that requires escapism.

It doesn't help that Alex has been so amazing about Dad — what can she do *but* obsess over him when he insists upon such sensitivity and tact? They were together when she found out — aren't they always together? She'd have rejected the call when 'Mum' came up on the screen if it wasn't the case that her mother very rarely tries to call her. Her initial impulse was to think something had happened to Gemma or Matthew. That's how she answered: 'What's wrong? Are Gemma and Matthew okay?' She wondered afterwards if her mother was offended that Anna hadn't urgently enquired after *her* well-being, or if she understood things better than Anna was giving her credit for. Her mother is difficult to predict — an intelligent woman, prone to self-sacrifice, nevertheless capable of a hysterical narcissism. The way she reacts is not always grounded in logic or reason. Anna had wondered, even as she answered, if her opening gambit would be a sufficient catalyst for a meltdown, if she would ever get to hear the real reason for the call, or if she would instead be subjected to a forty-five-minute tirade about her own reprehensible heartlessness, all because her initial concern was for her siblings and not for her long-suffering mother.

That's the kind of thing that used to happen, back before they reached their relatively amicable entente.

Her mother, in this instance, chose peace. She was even quite kind, given that it must have been strange to be the less-favoured parent, bringing news of the favoured parent's death.

'No, no, don't panic – Gemma and Matthew are fine.' She delivered this with crisp efficiency, which Anna appreciated. She and Alex were sitting in a beer garden in Dulwich, and at this juncture she briefly loosened her grip on his arm. She didn't say anything, not wanting to postpone whatever news had provoked this infringement on her time. Her mind went to Amy, to Buoy, to the house on Gollan Hill. It didn't occur to her that her mother was still, despite everything, her primary conduit to him.

'It's your father. Your father's dead, Annie. He died.'

Anna used to joke to her friends that her mother had the worst bedside manner. She never seemed to have any interest in softening the blow of difficult information – everything was administered with the same serrated tone, often with repetitions, to ensure you got the message, to preclude any chance of confusion. Anna always wondered what her mother was like with the families of lymphoma sufferers, if she was gentle, and if that was the problem – maybe she used up all her compassion on them. She's a popular woman, Anna's mother, for some reason: she has loads of friends from work and university and volunteering. How does she deliver bad news to them? Was it only Anna and her father who got irritable dispassion?

She listened to her mother relay the details of her wonderful, strange, disconnected father's expiry, as she sat in a Dulwich beer garden, watching the sun brand the chromatic sky with its hot trail, clinging to the arm of the man she thinks she might already be in love with. Alex looked at her, his brow sagging with uncertain concern. She looked at him, incapable of conveying anything with her features.

The information was both real and not real, upon receipt. She'd thought about her parents dying before, lots of times – you have to, right? Because they will, because they do. She'd cried at completely inappropriate moments, on trains or at the gym, purely because the thought of one of them being gone had arrived, unprompted. While the tears tended to arrive a little quicker in relation to her father, she liked that the tears always came. It made her feel that, despite everything, she had a normal and healthy attachment to the people who had made her. The tears weren't real though, was the thing, and the bodily response to this moment of voluntary misery fodder wasn't a marker of emotional health. She imagined how appalled her mother would be at being implicated in such pointless behaviour, and she was always a bit disgusted at herself, afterwards, for fetishising her own hypothetical bereavement.

And it turns out the reality was nothing like she'd imagined, anyway, because she didn't cry, at first. She didn't do much of anything, at first. It turned out there was some horrible capacity within her for utter inertia in the face of news like this, some automatic deployment of redundancy. Her mind flooded with a cold anaesthetising chemical, holding her in a blank state of utter non-responsiveness.

'Anna?' No more 'Annie' – her mother had quickly pivoted into logistician mode, ushering the conversation towards efficiency.

She wondered if her mother was deriving some satisfaction from telling her eldest daughter about the death of her father. The poetic justice of the moment can't have been lost on her, for hadn't her mother spent most of Anna's adolescence telling her that her faith in her father was misplaced? That she'd backed the wrong horse, idolised the wrong parent? Wasn't her mother always telling her that he was unreliable, that he had issues she was too young and stupid to understand? Surely there was a kind of vindication for her mother in all this, because wasn't this just another instance of his leaving? Hadn't he *always* left them?

Anna felt the impulse to challenge her, then. She wanted to say to her mother, over the phone, 'You're loving this, aren't you?' She wanted to bleed the full, years-accumulated reservoir of her anger. She wanted to show her mother that she has always had the full measure of her.

She didn't, though. You can't reinflate a burst balloon, and besides, the thought arrived abstractedly, she only had one parent now. She continued to say nothing. She didn't ask how Yvonne was, nor did she ask how Gemma and Matthew were taking it, because *her* father didn't belong to them – they didn't know him the way she did. She felt a different strain of her anger picking at her concentration, and because anger was a more familiar companion than whatever this new feeling was, she focussed on it. She absented herself from participation in the conversation, hummed her way through the details. When the details had run out, she said, 'Thanks for letting me know,' as though she were speaking to her landlord, and then she ended the call. She told Alex that her father was dead, and neither of them had to wonder how he might have coped with a messy, public display of weeping, because it turned out she was the one who couldn't stomach the drama of it. She cried in a small way, like a leaking valve. Alex held her hand and asked what she needed, and she said she needed a drink, so he got her a drink, and then another drink. When the bar closed, they got a bus back to his flat in Blackheath, and she booked a flight home. At one in the morning, just as they were about to dispatch the ends of the bottle of Jameson's, she realised she was now living in the day after the day she discovered her father was dead. She tried to articulate this thought with brusque detachment, but her voice failed on the penultimate word, and she stopped herself from forcing it, not sure what she was risking shaking loose along with the language. Alex said nothing, just waited, and a moment later a different thought came, a thought she didn't even attempt to externalise because of how immediately ashamed she felt for thinking it, how despicable she felt for giving in to her own self-aggrandising... How could he do this, to her? With no explanation? How could he leave her like this?

She sobbed then, finally. She sobbed at herself, at how cruel she could be. Alex held her, and eventually her sobs turned to rapid and soggy inhalations, and finally she took a breath that introduced the promise of a second, more normal breath. She didn't tell Alex what she'd been thinking, because she knew he would forgive her, and she didn't want forgiveness, she wanted to inhabit fully her own cruelty, because it seemed the only way to embody what was true, which was that her dad was dead, and she blamed him for being so. After everything, he'd proven her mother right.

Throughout the night, and the following day, she was grateful for Alex's existence, for how his presence helped her retreat from the frightening clarity of her anger. He bolstered her resolve not to succumb to the worst impulses of her emotional animal. Around him, she worked to perform her grief in conventional ways. She was grateful, not just because he was trying so hard to comfort her, but because his being there enabled her to keep most of her focus on the mission at hand – the mission of securing his unfaltering attention.

Gemma is thumping her uncertain way up the stairs. There are leaden feet on the landing, then a miscalculated bang of her bedroom door. Anna laughs, and her phone voot-voots again. Alex is listening to Big

Thief on his walk home – he sends her the Spotify link to 'Paul', and she scrabbles among the shadows on her bedroom floor for her headphones. She listens along, investing the gesture with an intimacy she can feel in her bones.

"As I realised there was no one who could kiss away my shit" he quotes.

That's a killer line she writes.

Speaking of he follows up, and she sighs heavily into the silence of the room as the song continues to play in her ears. The fantasy fractures. She knows what's coming.

I'm wondering if we should try and slow down a bit he says.

She moves her thumbs with a slow deliberation, as though they are dogs in need of training. Okay she says. You know I'm happy to take this at whatever pace works for you She has always been good at feigning the posture of understanding.

The problem is he writes, I don't know if I know how to take things slow with you. I just want to be with u all the time

Well she says, That's very easily arranged

Hahaha

The way to coax a man is to become his flirtatious lickspittle – offer him everything he might want, but with the tone of a temptress. She needs to pretend that he is an addict, she a sybarite, luring him in with the promise of pleasure.

But he adds. The problem is that I still feel very sad about Beth And there it is, the ex's name in Anna's childhood bedroom, ominous as the monsters she used to imagine in the dark corners. Maybe all the entities she ever conjured to frighten herself as a child were just early prototypes for what would one day become the real threat to her serenity: a man's devotion to his own feelings.

She wonders if she has ever, as an adult, felt as sad about anything as enlightened men seem to feel about everything. As a teenager she was taught by television that men were cold, brittle, unfeeling sorts, forced to endure their mercurial feminine counterparts. Her experience of recent years has been the opposite – women press forward with practicality, jettisoning the dead weight of rumination at the earliest opportunity. Meanwhile, men demand space to wallow and weep.

It's her own fault, she supposes, for running with gangs of artistic types – sentiment is paramount, both as a generative highway towards creative production, but also as a righteous affront to typical masculine values. If men have been taught by history not to feel, then it is the duty of good men to feel energetically, to become acolytes of sorrow. The problem with this new curriculum is that whoever designed it abandoned it halfway through, for while these men have become admirable scholars of their own emotional introspection, they've not gotten as far as acknowledging anyone else's.

She knows this isn't a fair assessment, really – Alex is almost overbearing in his insistence that she speak her mind. He's *desperate* to platform her thoughts and experiences. The main issue is he won't allow for the fact that Anna doesn't *want* a platform. Being listened to is appealing in the abstract, but she was raised to appreciate that not everything she thinks is worthy of being vocalised. It's the one thing her mother got definitively right, investing Anna with a healthy disdain for her own feelings. If a feeling can be dealt with quietly, or at least relegated to some less-attended-to part of her conscious mind, then it ought to be. Not *every* impulse needs a summit, not *every* emotion deserves an outing.

I get it she replies. It would be weird if you didn't feel sad, you were together for a long time.

I just don't want to hurt you in the process of getting over her – obviously I don't want to stop seeing you, but I'm worried that while I'm still processing the break-up, I won't be able to commit to this in the way that it deserves.

It's aggravating, how much sense he's making. Within the exhaustively defined parameters of his current emotional state, his conclusion is clearly the correct one. It just also happens to be the conclusion that thwarts Anna's most immediate want, which is the totality of his devotion, his happy acquiescence to their obvious well-suitedness. Wretchedly, his caution is a symptom of the same condition that makes her so besotted with him – the condition of his being perfect.

Yeah she says.

She wonders what he would think if he could see her now, regressed and babyish in this tiny bed, participating in so mature and candid a conversation as this. When she was a teenager, she and her best friend Louise would carefully workshop messages to send to the boys in their class, and over the years she's conducted lazy correspondence with various guys during various visits home, but Alex is so different from that, he wields a much greater conceptual heft. He's thirty-three, a smoker, a Tesco Clubcard holder. He and Anna have adult sex, with all of adult sex's sexless bureaucracy: they pick up boxes of Durex on trips to the supermarket, which loll in the basket with tenderstem broccoli and tins of baked beans. She issues instructions, mid-touch, to secure her own pleasure, while he had an STI check before their first date. She diligently pisses after every bout, even though the walls of his en suite are flimsy and not at all soundproof. To be corresponding with *this* man, specifically, in this tiny, springy bed, the place that once housed all her ideations of what life might be like, feels perverse. She can't shake a certain wariness – the thick folds of time compress like those of fire bellows, threatening to squash her among them. She never even had a boy in this room as a teenager, and now here she is, talking a hairy petit maître down from the cliff of his anguish.

Leaving home at sixteen was a bit of a gaffe, in some respects. She made everything harder for herself (though when has she not done this?). The problem was, she'd backed herself into a corner with her mother, and her statements were rapidly becoming blunted by the frequency of their deployment. It had been three years since Dad had drifted off to America without her, and she couldn't very well threaten to go live with him, especially when no invitation was forthcoming. All she could do was say she didn't want to be *there*, at home, on Gollan Hill, and after the tenth or so time she declared this, her mother simply gestured to the door. By the end, her options were submit or revolt, and though she probably could have borne two more years of her mother's tyranny, for the sake of getting some more qualifications, it seemed the much more glamorous option to stage a mutiny. So, she left. Her mother obviously assumed she would never do it, which is why she had to do it. During the briefest of caesuras, while her mother was taking a night off from ladling out generalised discontent to have dinner with some of her weird uni mates, Anna loaded up her fraying sports bag with jumpers and jeans. She got Louise to persuade her older brother Ross to drive out to Gollan to pick her up, then she stayed at Louise's for two days. She told her mother she'd be back by Sunday night, to which her mother responded, 'It'll be good for us to get some space from each other.' Rather than returning home, Anna caught a bus to Belfast on Sunday morning. From the relative safety of the Glenshane Pass, she composed a lengthy text, informing her mother that she wouldn't be returning. When the phone started ringing, she simply turned it off, feeling like a heroine outlaw in a film.

Ross had friends at Queen's with a spare bed, in a room too small to be legally listed by the landlord as a viable living space. This became Anna's oubliette of righteousness, her independence dungeon. The house was just off Ulsterville Avenue, and everyone Anna saw was either a student or a tourist on an open-top bus. Connected to the patchy Wi-Fi, Anna sent her father a succession of emails, informing him of her great escape. She liked that the practical circumstances of their lives were now knit closer, that she had proved herself woven from the same mental fabric as him, for hadn't he staged his own, similar escape, years earlier? They were now freshly allied, and wasn't her decampment a kind of inheritance? Weren't they both veterans, defecting from the regime of her mother? The transatlantic time difference meant his replies came at antisocial hours, and she loved to wake up in the morning to see his name on her laptop screen, a litany of jolly quips stamped with 3 a.m. Among his silly observations about new film releases and 'Yank ways of doing things' were repeated reminders to eat enough, to stay warm, to stay in touch. It was a kind of parenting that had never been demanded of him, it having always been Anna's mother who was responsible for the daily conditions of her survival. Her childhood memories of her father were composed largely of his confusing, roving stories – of fantastical worlds he created for her to stamp through. He had never been the worrying parent, and even though this specific genre of long-distance nurture asked little of him, practically speaking, Anna was nevertheless moved that he'd taken to it with so much gusto, and with none of the put-upon martyrdom that had always defined her mother's approach to caregiving.

That period of Anna's life was marked by surreality – she woke up each morning with a temporary amnesia, expecting to be back on Gollan, late for school. She approached everything as though she were an extra in an RTE drama, performing a load of laundry and then glancing around as though to confirm with the director that she'd been convincing. She bought loaves of Hovis like a tour guide, demonstrating how to assimilate to a gaggle of French teenagers. It was all so removed from anything she'd experienced before, so far from what she'd expected this period of her life to look like, that she couldn't quite relax into it. She applied for jobs, and got one in Debenhams as part of their rapacious, pre-Christmas uptake. She'd wake to the allegretto of her phone alarm at 7 a.m. every morning, then catch the bus into town in time for her shift. She didn't mind the early starts – because she had no real friends, her lifestyle was suited to both regiment and frugality. One of the girls in the house was a second-year English Lit student, who granted Anna access to her bookshelves.

Anna spent most of the year fighting her way through *Moby Dick* with a tin of Carlsberg, curled up on the damp sofa. She contributed her minimum wages to bills and beer, never checking her bank balance but also never needing to – she'd become so professional with her parsimony that money always appeared when she summoned it from the ATM. She was proud of herself – her budgeting was clearly brilliant.

It was a while later that she realised her father was depositing money into her bank account every month. This stoked an internal conflict, because on the one hand she would sooner have died than reject her awkward dad's gesture of love, but on the other, she thought she'd been doing a rather rousing turn as a plucky urchin and how dare his rescue mission dispel that. She wanted more than anything to be the self-made hero of her own narrative, and she's loath, even now, to admit that this was never really the case.

She resumed a very limited kind of correspondence with her mother about two months after she left, thanks to many coaxing emails, and calls, and aggressively jovial visits from Amy. Anna had never been quite sure how to take Amy – she was, at times, a cartoonish cameo, popping up when comic relief was needed. She has also always had a singular propensity for smugness, of which Anna thinks writing poetry must be either the cause or the symptom. She had a long-term girlfriend for a while – a very beautiful Butch called Jess – who one day, for unknown reasons, was no longer in the picture, and about whom Anna was discouraged from asking. In her singledom, Amy has become somehow even more like a woman in a tampon commercial, all empty aphorisms and easy feminism. During those first months when Anna was in Belfast, Amy elected herself mediator between the two warring factions, and to her credit she was almost too canny, *too* good at the job, because she never tried to proselytise Anna, never tried to convince her that her behaviour had been rash or that her mother's had been reasonable. Instead, she declared Anna an iconoclast, spun a narrative wherein the two of them were comrades in arms, resistant to the staid, predictable ways most people lived their lives. Anna wasn't sure if she necessarily wanted to be inducted into this elite club of two, but she couldn't resist co-authoring the saga of self, in which she was not immature, or petulant, but feisty and tenacious. Maybe she *had* taken charge of her own destiny. Amy let her pontificate for hours over tiramisu in posh Italian restaurants, and because Amy resembled, in minuscule ways, Anna's mother, these conclaves were almost as cathartic as being able to communicate her fury directly. In some ways more cathartic, even, because Amy didn't retaliate in the way Yvonne would have. Despite her lofty appraisals, Amy was nevertheless able to make Anna feel listened to, and Anna was almost appalled at how quickly the shrine she'd erected to her own dissatisfaction began to crumble. One day, at Amy's behest, she sent her mother a brief, cordial text: Hi Mum, how are things? I'm doing well, I have a nice room in a houseshare with nice people – friends of Louise's brother, you know Ross? I got a job in Debenhams and everything's fine.

Anna knew her mother had all this information already, that Anna wouldn't have been allowed the tranquillity of the last few months if her mother had not deemed tolerable the conditions of her rebellion. It was important to Anna that she pretend this wasn't the case, though – the infusions of money from her father aside, she needed to feel like the choices she'd made belonged to her entirely, that they weren't just the quirks of some experiment, at the helm of which her mother continued to preside.

Whether Amy had briefed her mother on Anna's needs in this regard, or whether her mother had opted via her own volition for generosity, the response came with the right arrangement of words, with the correct commitment to the fantasy: Hi Anna. It's nice to hear from you. It sounds like you're doing very well. All fine here. Gemma has decided she wants to learn the piano, and Matthew took a tumble playing rounders, but nothing too serious. They're both asking after you.

The text seemed to crackle off the screen with the force of its composition's effort – it took Anna nearly a day to decipher it. This new language between them was one of painfully contrived civility, and Anna couldn't decide if it was hilarious or tragic.

In early November, another text came in: Hi Anna. I know work must be very busy, what with the run-up to Christmas, but I was wondering if you might have a weekend evening free sometime soon? If so, would you like to come home to stay for a night?

At the time, Anna was reading a beaten-up copy of *No Man's Land*, and she couldn't help but think that a lot of that first visit home felt a bit like Pinter, but hack. She and her mother behaved like aggressively cordial automatons, exchanging forced niceties, misunderstandings, apologies.

'Would you like a glass?'

'Uh, sure, but I can just grab one from the cupboard here. Thanks.'

'I meant of this.'

'What?'

'The wine.'

'Oh, sorry. I didn't spot it.'

'Would you like a glass?'

'Are you sure?'

'Or there's beer?'

'No, wine would be lovely. Thank you.'

'It's not very chilled though. Sorry about that.'

'Is it not red?'

'What's that, sorry?'

'The wine, isn't it red?'

'No, it's white.'

'Oh, sorry, just – the bottle – the bottle is dark. I thought white wine normally came in see-through bottles.'

'I think I have some red, somewhere, if you'd prefer it? Sorry, I should have thought.'

'No, sorry, white is perfect. I just thought it was red.'

'Sorry, yes, no, it's white.'

'What kind?'

'Sorry?'

'What sort of wine is it?'

'Oh, sorry. My head's turned. It's sauvignon. Is that okay?'

'Of course! That's lovely – not even sure why I asked. Thank you.'

'But there is beer if you'd prefer. I think it's IPA, if you like that.'

'No, wine is perfect — sorry, it was just the colour of the bottle that confused me.'

'Yes, I'm not sure why it's in a dark bottle.'

'Are the wine glasses in the dishwasher?'

'They should be in the cupboard. Sorry, I'll get it.'

'No, sorry, I —'

Throughout this pantomime, an eight-year-old Gemma sat at the table, frowning at a sudoku while Amy plaited her hair and rolled her eyes. Anna felt embarrassed that all her righteous indignation had been reduced to this, sputtering nonsense at her equally flustered mother. It all felt so anticlimactic, but then the weeks spent filibustering Amy over fancy desserts had effectively dulled her wrath. More than anything, now she just felt tired. She didn't want to charge back onto the battlefield, to reignite the torch of their acrimony. She wanted, and perhaps this was the only thing she had ever wanted, to talk to her mother like an old confidante — she wanted to gossip about her line manager with the mad teeth; she wanted to offer to cook, to show off her new self-sufficiency. This new dynamic, it turned out, wasn't hilarious; it was lonely.

* * *

The worst part came when she had to leave, to go back to the sodden closet of her sovereignty, and renounce the pleasures of home: the clean floor, the fragrant bathroom, the soft faces of her perfect younger siblings. At the door, her mother's face was screwed up into something unreadable, her hands flapping at her sides like ill-conceived semaphores. It took Amy, once again, to correct things: 'Come on girls, hug it out.' Anna tried to read her mother's crowded expression – love, anguish, pride and anger all competed for dominion. She held out her arms, dutifully, and Anna hated that her mother viewed this whole display as an admission of defeat, because that's precisely how Anna viewed it, and she didn't want them to be the same, she didn't want them to both view their participation in the visit as a magnanimous capitulation – Anna wanted to be the sole forgiver, the sole redeemer. They couldn't *both* be the bigger person.

What she learned a second later, though, was that the discomfort of this feeling had nothing on the one that followed, which came when she stepped into her mother's arms, and felt her mother's long, strong hands on her shoulder blades. She felt immediately the layered echoes of a life's worth of similar embraces, the whole great history of her mother's complicated protection. The weight and fullness of biology pressed the air from her lungs, and just as a hatred of the visit's formal demands had reckoned with all Anna's other feelings over the last day and a half, now a hatred of her own weakness did battle with her physiognomic response, because suddenly Anna was crying, and she couldn't stop. She pressed her arms into her mother's torso and sobbed helplessly into her shoulder, because there hadn't been a moment in Anna's seventeen years of life that had not orbited around *this* body, this person, this mind, and for all of her posturing and sedition and genuine distaste for how frequently this woman had taken advantage of that orbit, her mother was, nevertheless, the only being alive who could offer this precise flavour of comfort, this promise of safety.

Predictably, perhaps, this moment did not mark any radical change in how either Anna or her mother conducted themselves. It heralded a brief armistice, wherein Anna stopped jeopardising her future to prove a point, and her mother stopped pushing the agenda that every small transgression perpetuated by Anna, past and present, was tantamount to Armageddon. She even resisted weaponising Anna's departure, which Anna was genuinely impressed by, because she knew there was no piece of rhetoric more seductive to her mother than the idea that Anna was *exactly* like her father'.

Anna did not return home – it was too important to her that leaving had not been exclusively a reactionary tactic – but she did permit her mother a more explicit influence, and within weeks of the new year's commencement she was enrolled on an Access Course, was sleeping in a real bedroom in a different, nicer house-share, and was attending a weekly book club at the Crescent Arts Centre. A year and a half later, she started her literature degree at Queen's, replete with her former housemate's entire collection of course texts. Four years later, she started a master's degree at the University of Ulster, and five and a half years later she was in London, working as a copywriter and aspiring critic, living in Brockley with a PA and aspiring actor, and a theatre usher and aspiring screenwriter.

Throughout all of this, her mother substituted intimacy for pragmatic discussions with Anna's father about the need to support her financially. By insisting upon giving Anna money, her mother was able to provide for her, while simultaneously implying that Anna wasn't fit to provide for herself. Even now that Anna is twenty-six, her mother seems set on belittling her at every opportunity, be it over her outfits, her career or her politics. She thinks Anna's nationalism is a lazy and reactionary capitulation to populist rhetoric; she thinks Anna's outfits are unflattering and her work is shallow and vacuous. Neither respects the other's value system, but while Anna knows that her mother's way of thinking is archaic and stolid, her mother assumes Anna's is the result of a gullible mind. They still cannot have a conversation about anything political without bickering, and neither of them can bicker for long without resorting to personal attacks. Anna tries to avoid getting drawn in, not wanting to find herself in a situation where she has to apologise for being honest.

The party where Anna met Alex took place in a home with walls littered with appalling art – mutilated Mickey Mouses, rendered in thick black ink, cavorted across a watercolour pastoral; a Chagall-style goat lay prostrate on a Lichtenstein colour scheme. Anna didn't know the man who was hosting the party, and even after attending the party she did not know the man who was hosting the party. The loose theme of the guest list was 'industry people', but this was porous enough to permit anyone with sufficient social cachet. Anna was there as a guest of her friend Lucy, an editorial assistant and aspiring assistant editor.

They each did a line of coke in a pub toilet beforehand, and within ten minutes of meeting Alex, Anna was performing paragraphs of Sally Rooney's *Normal People*, had it been written by D. H. Lawrence.

'Connell's chain glistened with all the orgiastic poverty of bitumen. Marianne realised, with all the magnitude of a life's uneasy regret, that the fatted boils of her loneliness might be lanced by this necklace's unfaltering links. She thought of its edges slithering over her brittle flesh like some happy snake, and the ranting idiot of her cunt opened its mouth to Connell's moonish gaze.'

Alex had done his PhD on Lawrence, and was therefore the best and worst possible person to receive this performance. He visibly despised this coked-up lunatic, squealing at him in a boggy front garden, and yet he couldn't stop laughing. The night ground on around them, and never had Anna experienced a dance of this type – they oscillated between perfect accord and violent disagreement, they found the middle ground and then set fire to it.

Lucy had promised Anna that the party would be good for her career, that it was the perfect place to meet commissioning editors and authors and kingpins. Instead, Anna went home with a lecturer in twentieth-century literature, perhaps the only person

ANNA

at the party with less influence than her. She immediately stopped messaging Jack and threw herself wholeheartedly into this new fixation, telling herself that Alex's baggage was no deterrent to what was so clearly a fated attraction.

> I'm sorry he says now. I know this is so much to put on you at 2 a.m. I'm just drunk and I miss you but I don't know how best to approach this
> There's no one who can kiss away your shit
> EXACTLY
> I don't think we have to solve this right now
> You're probably right
> I am right, and you're just being a drunk and silly goose
> Hawnk
> Exactly
> When are you coming back?
> I'm not sure – I took a week's leave, so a couple of days after the funeral, I guess
> Ah, Christ, fuck. I'm such a dickhead. I can't believe I'm making you think about this bullshit when you're burying your fucking dad
> To be fair, I think these days you hire someone else to do the actual burying
> Hahaha

I'm mostly sitting on my arse

Pretty lazy of you, frankly

It is lazy of me, and don't call me Frankly

Hahaha

Seriously, the least I can do is counsel you through some turmoil – it's a pretty welcome distraction

I feel incredibly strongly about you, I hope you know that

She swallows an *I love you*. That's nice to hear she says.

Come straight to mine from the airport, when you get back. I'll make you dinner

Okay

I just got home so I'm gonna crash

Okay

Gotta turn my moonish gaze bedwards

Hahaha

Night xxx

xxx

She rolls over in bed and tries to look at the dark. Her eyes close against its intensity, and she starts picturing what she would wear, if they got married. A simple slip dress with an oversized tuxedo jacket, maybe. A low heel – mules? A bright colour might look good…

She forces her thoughts from the impulse, sickened with herself. The fading images of soft curls and plaited wedding bands prompt her to reilluminate her phone screen. She composes a text and sends it. She casts her phone from her body.

She never really expected her father to take her with him to America. She knew, had always known on some level, that he just wasn't fit for it – parenting wasn't his natural métier. She shouldn't have asked to go with him, because it forced them all to pretend that it was her mother's interdiction, rather than her father's uncertainty, that prevented it. At thirteen, she had no interest in hating both her parents, because that would have undermined the legitimacy of the project; she'd have seemed histrionic and typically adolescent. The impingements upon her liberty had always been delivered in her mother's voice, and so her mother was always the jailer. It was easier to continue to commit to this idea than acknowledge the truth – that her mother was just a parent, albeit a difficult one. Her dad was a gentler, benign presence – as capable of raising her as an imaginary friend would have been. Anna couldn't bear turning her ire upon him, and so the myth of her mother's tyranny was germinated, nurtured, extended. Had her mother ever softened in the years following her father's departure, there might have been cause for an edit, but she stayed recalcitrant, and so Anna remained stubborn. This is their internecine war – they are two puritans on either side of an unscalable wall, both too proud to acknowledge that the wall is a curtain.

Anna wonders what will become of her mother, now Dad is gone. How does she feel about any of it? She won't stop banging on about this dinner she's planning, after the funeral. Hearing her agonise yesterday afternoon about the ingredients and the menu and the itinerary, you'd think it was going to be some kind of revolutionary occasion, rather than something that has happened a thousand times before. That must be symptomatic of something, surely. Some kind of mad displacement activity. Maybe she's feeling pressure to be better, now that she's the only one to whom deathbed recriminations can be directed. Maybe she thinks this roast dinner will herald in a new era: family 2.0.

It's not the case, really, that Anna ever loved her father more – she liked him more, because he never gave her cause to wish him ill. Even in the period around Matthew's birth, when he was more a heap of thinly draped pulleys and whistles than a man, she could tell he loved her. Every day, she watched him summon love from a wrecked receptacle. Matthew and Gemma weren't yet alive enough to witness or participate in this exchange, and so Anna got to feel uniquely suited to adoring him, even when he was like this. Time and time again she reached through the mire to find her father, and once he was better there remained a singular correspondence between them, a love she didn't wish to complicate with anger. She loved him in a way that felt endlessly forthcoming and uncomplicated, that she never had to question the parameters of. His failures felt easy to forgive, unlike her mother's, and she loved him even more for letting her feel mature in so readily accepting his limitations. What those limitations were, now she thinks about it, was never fully explained – he was just her dad. He was remote and spectral and subject to forces she didn't understand, but he was also gentle and kind, completely without anger. She loves her mother with the kind of intensity that incurs love's opposite, because the more foundational someone is in your life, the more scope there is for failure. Anna despises her mother because she forces Anna to occasionally want her dead, and when you love someone there's no impulse more shameful than the fantasy of their destruction.

She wakes at 7:30 with no alarm – a lingering side-effect of the Debenhams years. The house feels full with the torpor of sleeping bodies. She remembers her final message last night and tries to assess her feelings about having sent it, coming up blank. She curls her naked body into a sitting position, then she massages the weighty bloat of her full bladder. She gets out of bed and pulls tracksuit bottoms on over her bare skin, then a thin, gauzy vest top, which she knows her mother will hate. She opens her bedroom door and surveys the carnage left by Gemma – the welcome mat askew and discoloured with the pallor of sand, a set of keys akimbo on the floor. She checks the front door: unlocked. A sodden pile of something seeps beneath the radiator, clearly having slipped down under its own weight during the night. Anna approaches it gingerly, then plucks the dense anemone from the floor. It's a red, furry hoodie, soaked to a maroon colour. As she lifts it, drops of water fall in a determined shower.

'Shit,' she mutters. She returns it to the floor and darts into her room. She gathers up a consortium of half-dirty clothes in her arms, then delivers them to the utility room, piling them into the washing machine. She returns for the hoodie, wadding it into a plastic bag for transport. She carries the soggy albumen to the machine, then sets it to a wash-dry cycle. She attacks the hall floor with kitchen roll, mopping up the puddle. She opens the front door and thumps the welcome mat into the cool morning air; it sends a flurry of pale granules onto the wind's current. She locks the door and returns to the kitchen, disposing of the saturated mass of paper towels. On the counter is a ravaged pot of Tesco Finest houmous and an empty packet of Walkers, surrounded by crisp bits and pale beige blobs. She dips a finger in the houmous pot and sucks it, then gets started on cleaning up the mess. Buoy, uncharacteristically docile during these proceedings, finally lifts her shaggy head from bed and looks at her.

'Hi snuffles – you okay?'

Buoy says nothing, and after a few moments she returns her snout to whatever secreted treasure has kept her so transfixed throughout Anna's clean-up. Anna then notices the object in bed with the small dog. She curls her nose, approaches cautiously.

'What's that, Boo?' Buoy wags her tail in expectation. Anna bends and frowns, unable to interpret the components of what's in front of her. After a moment, she recognises the raw, half-eaten chicken, nestled into the cushion of Buoy's bed like a whelped pup. The chewed plastic wrapper lies in a putrid heap on the kitchen tile. Anna's stomach rotates, she suppresses a gag.

'Jesus fucking Christ.'

She glides from the kitchen into the utility room, then glances at the garage door. The keys hang in the lock. The door is ajar.

'Oh. Fuck.'

She steps gingerly onto the cold cement floor, the silhouettes of long-neglected bicycles looming at her from the corners. She approaches the huge fridge like it's a sleeping behemoth, opens it tenderly, just in case some strange and unlikely miracle has taken place. It hasn't. The much-vaunted chicken, the centrepiece of Monday night's grand dinner, is no longer in the drawer. Gone, also, is the fancy houmous. She turns back to look at Buoy, who has followed her, no doubt in pursuit of further windfalls. She pants in blithe contentment, seemingly invulnerable to the huge quantity of raw chicken she has consumed.

Anna wraps her hands in her hair and shakes her head slowly in disbelief.

'What the fuck happened here, Boo? How did you get in there? How did you get that?'

Buoy says nothing, merely watches her. She sighs.

'Right, okay. Fucking Gemma. Fuck.'

She works quickly. She locks the garage door, returns the keys to their bowl on the counter. She takes a plastic bag from the cupboard under the kitchen sink and wraps it around one hand. She extricates the chicken from Buoy's bed with a professional delicacy, pushing Buoy's belligerent nose out of the way. Holding the bagged chicken aloft, she paces. The kitchen bin is too obvious, ditto the wheelie bin outside – her mother has an impossible acuity for all things amiss. She hears a rumble from upstairs. Someone is awake. 'Fuck,' she whispers under her breath. She canters to her bedroom with the bagged chicken – the only space over which she has total control. She places the carcass in the small, white bin under her desk, then sprays Prada perfume into the air. That'll have to do for now.

She returns to the kitchen, closing her bedroom door behind her. Buoy is still in bed, looking wounded.

'Sorry, Boo.'

She puts the kettle on and checks her phone. She has a new message: Hey you, long time no see! I'm about tonight, what do you fancy doing? She blows air out of her cheeks, then places the phone face down on the counter. She falls forward into a downward dog position, allowing her thoughts to pool in the peak of her forehead. The kettle whistles, Buoy sneezes.

The evening sky is violet. The afternoon rain has diluted the clouds to near-transparency. Anna pulls a soft, split-hemmed cream jumper on, then swaps her tracksuit bottoms for high-waisted, oversized jeans which freeze in starchy folds around her shins and knees. She does her make-up in a mirror by the window, blending taupe pigment onto her cheekbones and around her jaw-line. She dabs blush hear her temples and at the outer corners of her eyes, then lines her lips with dusky pink. She brushes her hair into a taut ponytail, which she plaits. She puts a gold hoop in each of her various ear piercings, then stares at the face in the mirror. It is both beautiful and ugly.

She throws her body at the kitchen door jamb, then leans against it. Her mother and Amy are sitting at the table, drinking wine.

'I'm heading out.'

Her mother turns in her seat. 'You are not.' It's neither a question nor a statement, simply a symptom of this weekend's liminal uncertainty.

'Just to see a friend from school. I won't be late.'

The details clarify in her mother's frown. She gestures across the table. 'Your aunt just got here.' There is safety in implicating another.

'Like I said, I won't be late. Amy doesn't mind, do you?'

Amy laughs, and it is so familiar in its specificity that Anna's life once more wrinkles onto itself. This is the laugh Amy does when she is used in this way. The family rides over its difficulties on Amy's back, and Amy revels in bestowing grace.

'It's fine,' Amy decrees. 'On you go, we can catch up later.' She gives Anna's mother a look, then Anna a different flavour of look. Anna rolls her eyes, then turns. She closes the door on her mother's final, secret utterance.

An hour earlier, there'd been a knock on her bedroom door. Anna was lying on her bed, flipping the pages of a Rachel Cusk and hoping that Alex might message her. Amy was thumping about upstairs, and the household felt distended with the new arrival. Anna ignored the first knock, and when it was followed by another, more tentative knock, she knew it wasn't her mother.

'Yep?'

The door opened, and Gemma's small, knotty face appeared. Anna rolled onto her front and tented her book's spine. She waited. Gemma said nothing at first, rippling like a bubble on water's surface. Anna tried to keep the impatience out of her voice.

'What's up, Gem?'

Anna knows it's partially her own fault that Gemma is so nervous around her – what should be a genetically determined ease with one another has been stunted by Anna's absence and unpredictability. That said, Anna also suspects that Gemma might be quite strange. She was thrilled to hear her drunken roving last night, because it suggested that Gemma has begun behaving in an intuitive way, rather than her usual posture of quiet watchfulness. Gemma has always seemed to Anna like a tiny, parasitic anthropologist, feigning belonging as a means of gathering data. She slipped into Anna's room and closed the door with all the mannerliness of an effete butler, and Anna couldn't help but think about how she is almost certainly still a virgin.

'There's something on the beach,' Gemma announced at last, folding her hands into her sleeves.

'Okay. What is it?'

'Like a big, ship thing.'

'A big, ship thing.'

'A shipwreck, maybe. Or a bit of one. On the beach.'

'Oh yeah? Cool.'

'I think it must have washed up from the sea.'

'Wow, that's fun. So did you check it out last night, then?'

'A bit, but uh, not much. I didn't, like, go inside it.'

'Okay, well maybe you can show me it tomorrow or something, yeah? I've actually got to get ready now, Gem – I'm heading out, so if you wouldn't mind –'

'Should – do you think I should tell Mum? Just, like, might it be dangerous?'

She had the wan, viscous sheen of an especially nasty teen hangover. She chewed on each idea with a slow effort, as though her thalamus was struggling to squeeze its offerings through cling film. Anna felt grateful that she's never had to navigate the precarities of a Gollan Hill Saturday with that specific flavour of next-day, pained disorientation. Her gratitude was twinned with something else, though, something ungenerous and mean, because she knows that their mother's tolerance of Gemma's hangover is indicative of a dwindling regime, a regime that

Anna has rarely been offered any reprieve from. She hopes Gemma and Matthew know how lucky they have it, blessed with being too young to have witnessed the years around their father's departure and subsequent announcement of glamorous Sasha, when every breath Anna took felt like a crime, when her mother's annihilating anger was hungry for any viable target. Gemma might think things are difficult now, but Anna saw the ruins this new, cagey peace was built on.

She doesn't *want* to be resentful of Gemma, though. She wants to be magnanimous. She wants to foster a natural, sisterly geniality. That's why she washed the hoodie and covered up the mess Gemma left in her wake – she wanted Gemma to see how badly she wants them to be on the same team. And maybe Gemma *does* see it, and maybe that's what provoked this: Gemma stood by Anna's dresser, oozing chemicals and agonising over phantom problems.

Anna pretended to give the question consideration, not wanting Gemma to feel stupid, even though the whole thing was stupid.

'No,' she said, trying to affect gravitas. 'Don't tell Mum – she'll just make it a whole thing. Things wash up on beaches all the time, it's not a big deal.'

Omission has always been one of Anna's preferred types of ammunition – one of the most satisfying means of rendering vulnerable the ties between two people, just as admission can achieve the opposite. By telling Anna, Gemma had forged an alliance between them, an alliance against their mother. Anna wondered if she could be a kind of second mother to her sister; a guardian against malign forces. She rather liked the idea.

Gemma had continued itching on the spot, clutching her hands. 'I'm just not sure if I should, you know, or if –'

'If you should what?'

'I don't know – just, if I –'

Anna watched her dither, increasingly impatient, increasingly unsympathetic.

'Don't worry about the chicken, by the way.' She hadn't planned on bringing it up, but then how many acts of charity should go unacknowledged?

Gemma had frowned. 'What?'

'The chicken you left out on the counter last night, which Buoy then proceeded to eat most of.'

They eyed one another. Anna watched the lost memory assemble itself in Gemma's eyes. A small, uncertain voice, 'Oh fuck.'

'Yep.'

'Oh fuck. Oh fuck oh fuck.'

'Bit drunk, were we? Bit snacky? Fancied some fancy houmous, did we? Forgot to put the chicken back in the fridge, did we?'

'Oh God, she's going to kill me.'

'Don't worry – I'll get a replacement when I'm out. We'll call in at McColgan's. She won't find out. Chill.'

More fretting. 'Oh God, what if she notices before then?'

'She won't. I'll sort it.'

'Oh God, are you sure?'

'I sorted the hoodie out, didn't I?' Another reckoning across Gemma's face. 'That was pretty weird too, by the way – what kind of mad night did you have?'

Gemma looked at her feet. Anna laughed.

'It'll all be fine, Gem. Now go away, I need to get ready.'

After Gemma left, tortured but partially comforted, Anna had an idea. She sent another text. Hey, do you want to come down to the beach first? We can take a walk, then go get a drink at the Railway after?

He replied instantly: That works. I'm just on my way now. See you soon x

ANNA

On the front step she tightens her plait, breathing deeply. She glances at the house behind her, wonders what her siblings are making of all this. The three of them have never been great at talking about things, it's more a 'look at this meme, have you seen this tweet' kind of relationship. They don't seem too devastated, but then death is quite abstract when you're young. They're lucky they weren't as close to Dad as she was. They won't be feeling what she's feeling, they won't have devoted the last week to armchair forensics in the way that she's been forced to. She runs her fingers down the loops of her plait, checking for escaping locks. She commences her descent to the beach.

She gets, or at least, she thinks she does, that it can't have been easy for either of her parents, living through the conflict. She's not the dilettante her mother thinks she is; she's read the books, listened to the takes. Reading isn't tantamount to living, though. Hearing about a thing doesn't equate to having felt it.

She knows, has always known, that things have been kept from her, but what infuriates her is that her mum then uses these omissions as an excuse to patronise, dismissing Anna for not understanding to a sufficiently 'nuanced' degree. Halfway down the steps she finds an errant bit of hair and tucks it into the weave, resisting the urge to stop and start the whole plait over. The sea rises to meet her. This evening is all that's in her control.

Rob is already in the car park, hunched over his phone. Anna bounds towards him, squinting at the freshly unveiled sun, throbbing on the horizon.

'Sure, there she is,' Rob says. He opens his arms and gathers her into a hug. She collapses against him, and their bodies compress. It lasts longer than is plausibly deniable. Finally, Anna steps back, and they evaluate one another. It's been years since they last met, but this has worked to both their advantages.

Rob was in the year ahead of her at school, now works in something nondescript and dull-seeming – one of those jobs that is just a succession of corporate nouns. He seemed intrigued to hear from her, which was good enough, because what she's craving is an evening fuelled by low-stakes novelty, something alien to her feelings for Alex, her feelings about Dad. She and Rob used to kiss on the steps of the Danske Bank in the Guildhall Square after under-age nights out. Her mother thought she was safely tucked in at Louise's, when Louise was in fact right around the corner, having the treasures of her groin excavated by her boyfriend. Anna is hoping that she and Rob will kiss tonight, that the temporal disorientation of the last few days might yield something pleasurable, might allow her to be sixteen again. Since Alex is so fixated on placing space between them, she might as well satisfy the criteria of their non-exclusivity. With that thought, she throws her arms around Rob once more. He tilts with the force of her. 'Oh, hey again,' he laughs into her hair. She tells him how well he looks.

He's not dressed for the beach, and there's an intermission while he unlaces his boots, removing them with the slow and resigned deliberation of someone given the wrong itinerary. Anna dances in one place, glancing repeatedly behind her, hoping Gemma's intel is accurate. When he's ready, they traverse the dunes, and as they make their way down to the beach she wonders if taking his hand in a display of girlish unsteadiness would be overkill. Her fingers wiggle next to his as she deliberates, but then they are on the flat, and the moment has passed. The shipwreck is there, where Gemma said it would be, the flaring grey flap of its fractured opening beckoning them to inspect it. It's not quite a full ship – more like a bit of one, but it's nevertheless much bigger than Anna expected. She's both relieved and a little unsettled. What if it's of greater significance than she assumed? She shakes her concerns away, using her plait as a leash to jerk her head to one side. She presents the marooned bit of hull to Rob with a flourish, 'Isn't it cool?'

He doesn't say anything at first. He approaches the wreck with caution, an indecipherable look on his face. He reaches a hand to touch the vessel's side, then elegantly sniffs his fingertips. Anna watches him steadily, as though he is the object, the artefact, the find. She's preparing to calibrate her reactions to his, because this is a one-night-only event – there isn't time for crossed wires or slack communications; they won't find their way to one another over weeks of study. He's here because she wants him. Tonight.

They never got any further than the sloppy, drunken kisses, and their correspondence has been infrequent and superficial over the years. She thinks he's a reliable bet for some lazy flirting, though – he's charming in a frivolous way, forgettably handsome. He likes going to the gym and accessorising his Mazda into ugliness. He wears tight jeans and has the tongues of a tattoo licking the neckline of his t-shirt. She wants tonight to be unscholarly and base, tactile and lusty – as disposable and merry as her relationship with Alex is complex. She thinks the shipwreck might be the key, might act as a catalyst: if she can provide novelty, then he'll want her. If she can be present at a moment of great anecdotal potential, how could he not want her?

As he stalks the shipwreck's perimeter, she ventures closer and lowers her body to the ground, using the fetid-smelling steel as back support. When Rob rounds the corner, she is there, smiling winningly up at him. 'This is so weird,' he laughs, and she pats the sand beside her. He asks, 'Do you think this thing is even safe? It's not going to, like, fall apart, or anything?' Now it's her turn to laugh. She tells him to live a little. She wiggles deeper into her groove, and in the molten scraps of the day's light the skin on the backs of her hands glows with a pungent femininity. Over the last couple of years she has finally begun to occasionally feel attractive, and it feels like a long overdue birthright, as an eldest daughter. For years, she couldn't understand her face – she couldn't judge which features were worthy of accentuation, which of concealment. The arrangement of her expression was too difficult, she was ill-equipped to assess its value. Finally, though, she's sussed it. While it's the case that the slightest mishap of light or colour can send her cascading into self-loathing, she has learned never to express those feelings, because what could be *less* sexy than low self-esteem? She obsesses as much over the tedium of her neuroses as the neuroses themselves, but what matters is that nobody knows. She wants people to think of her as above such insipid self-obsession; she wants Gemma to think of her as a role model, confident and sexually adventurous. She has decided, for both their sakes, to be exactly that.

Rob sits down next to her. He does a strange kind of smile, and she laughs again.

'I promise we'll go get a drink soon,' she says. 'I just thought this was pretty interesting, but it's totally okay if it's not your thing.'

She knows she has judged this statement correctly – Rob is the kind of man who wants to be thought of as more than the sum of his parts. He wants to be unpredictable amidst all the ways in which he is entirely predictable. If this shipwrecked bracket is out of keeping with what he might be thought to like, then he needs to like it.

'No, no,' he says quickly. 'I like it, it's kind of freaky. I wonder where it came from.'

'Right? And I wonder how long it was in the sea.'

'Yeah!' His smile settles into a more genuine one. While Anna knows that his willingness to indulge this woman he doesn't really know is not inexhaustible, he'll try for long enough to satisfy her needs, provided she can play the game. They eye each other, and then he shivers. She nudges her hips closer to his, puts one arm around him and the other hand on the thigh closest to hers. She rubs it, and they laugh at the ludicrousness of the arrangement: look, it's like she's the man! She thinks about what she might say next — their sporadic chat over the years has mostly been concerned with the material details of their lives.

'Did you ever go to Sunday School?' she says, brightly.

'What?'

'Sunday School — you know, the church club for little kids where you sing songs and hear Bible stories and stuff.'

'No, I didn't,' he smiles. 'We weren't big God people, funnily enough. Why were you thinking about that?'

She tells him that at Sunday School they were always singing a song about Jonah, who was thrown off a cargo ship and eaten by a whale. He's surprised that she went to Sunday School, and she thinks that this is promising, that there might be some scope for him to think of her as corruptible. He asks her if she believes in God, and she says that she thinks she does.

'Not in organised religion, obviously.' She imagines her mother listening in. 'I think lots of organised religion is just a carefully constructed excuse for hierarchical structures and bigotry.' She hopes she sounds clever. 'Jesus, though. Jesus, I like.'

She's offered him a means via which to tease her. He takes it. He asks her what it is that she likes about the magical man who couldn't die.

'Well, he was a socialist, you know? He was the *ultimate* socialist. He espoused ideas about equality and acceptance – plus, he beat the absolute shit into those moneylenders.'

Rob laughs. He continues the teasing. 'I mean, I'm not sure he actually espoused ideas about *anything*. I'm not sure he was real.'

She shoves him playfully. 'You know what I mean!' He wobbles on his sit bones, then settles back against her. She sighs.

'Plus,' she says, more quietly. 'He didn't think family was the be all and end all, you know?'

Anna knows from Louise that there was a lot of speculation about her departure from school, rumours of familial breakdown and estrangement. Louise, who at the time had wanted to become a lawyer, leaked the meaningless phrase 'civil emancipation' into the school corridors, thereby immortalising Anna as some kind of righteous objector. She's not sure how much Rob tuned into this lore, but she hopes he knows enough to think of her as wounded, in need of care. She sighs wistfully. He takes the bait. 'I'm sorry about your dad, by the way.'

'Yeah,' Anna says. 'Thanks.' She hadn't thought this through – her dad's face swims into shot. His eyes, green-tinged behind his glasses; almost empty until he smiled, when the skin of his temples and cheeks would concertina, thinning his irises to glinting slits. He was an easy laugh, or maybe that was just for her.

She's dismayed to find unhappiness encroaching on her seduction strategy. She feels the thickness in her sinuses, her nose eager to start dripping. She rolls her eyes and forces a cough, and nothing is said for a moment. She tries to reconstruct her composure, and when she's back in control she feels a wave of utter exhaustion. She hates that her dad is dead. She wants to go home. Silence sits between them for a moment.

'So,' Rob says. 'How did the Jonah song go?'

She sniffs herself back into the conversation. She's surprised at how good he is at this. It's a failure of imagination on her part, possibly, to assume that men who enjoy exercise lack social nuance, but she also thinks that it's probably true, and nothing Rob is doing is actually spectacular. She's just soft tonight, because she misses Alex, because she wants an easy tryst. Because her father is dead, and she doesn't understand why. She decides to sing the song for him, to reward his good behaviour. Her voice is horrible, as it always has been, but wouldn't singing be so much less intimate if she were good at it? At the song's close he applauds. She laughs, then shivers, and a restructuring occurs: he rescues her arm from his shoulder and places his around hers instead. She turns towards him, willing him to accept the cue. He does. They kiss. She opens her eyes at one point and the reflective hide of the shipwreck confuses her, so she closes them again. When their mouths come apart, she smiles.

'Want to go in and check it out?' she says.

'What?'

'In here,' she pats the hull's side. 'Shall we go in?'

'Why? Are you cold? If you're cold, we could just head to the pub.'

'I'm not cold,' she says.

'Then why do you want to –'

'Just,' she interrupts. 'It might be more private.' She looks fixedly at him, implying something with her eyes.

He thinks he's misinterpreted. 'Are you – are you serious?'

'Deadly.'

ANNA

She's getting it right, she thinks – she's showing him that she's complicated and desirable. She's bringing the wisdom of a decade of romantic disappointment to this brief, concentrated enticement. She's making herself the feminine ideal, the self-effacing conversationalist and the sexy maniac. It's insufficient to just be good company. You need something to muddy the waters of your affable personhood. You need to possess dangerous compulsions and remote vulnerabilities.

She stands and offers him her hand. He takes it, and when they are both upright, she puts her tongue to his lips. She licks his teeth. He responds to the stimulus, kissing her so hard that her spine curves. He puts his hand to the base of her back to keep her stationary while he adds more pressure. It's nothing like how it was, those nights by the Foyle when they were sticky and inexperienced.

The Foyle – she doesn't want to think about the Foyle.

She bites his bottom lip, then pulls away. He groans at the abruptness of the amnesty. She crosses her arms and takes her jumper off over her head, and in the soft light her erect nipples send thin shadows across her torso. She glances around to check that no errant beachcombers are in the vicinity, then she undoes her jeans and pushes them to ground. He reaches forward, but she tells him to wait. She beckons him towards the rusted flaps of the shipwreck's entrance. He asks, once more, if she's serious. She swivels her hips. She flaunts her debauchery.

Inside, the wreck smells of salt and decay. She holds her breath as they kiss, his bare chest against hers, his groin pressing her buttocks to the cold, sweating metal. She knows this was a good idea – that he will fantasise about this night in the future, reminiscing about the thrills only she can provide. As for Anna, she will go back to Alex a victor, with the confidence and equanimity of a goddess. If she can just secure this success, she will be able to secure him – she'll be self-assured, patient, composed. She won't disintegrate at his noble threats; she won't squall with need for him. They will build something real. She just needs to prove to herself that she's not weak.

Rob puts his thumb on her nipple, and she moans. The sound ricochets off the walls of the wreck. The floor is damp, with archipelagos of seaweed. They don't pursue the wreck to its full depths, staying close to the opening. They inch on their toes around the organic patches. In a relatively dry spot, they pause their waltz. She takes off her socks and he unbelts his jeans. As she pushes them to the floor and takes his cock in her grip, he retrieves a condom from his descending back pocket. They manoeuvre his cock inside her, commence thumping to the wall's sonorous judders. He cups the back of her skull with his hand to protect her head, then suggests they switch. They rotate 180 degrees, then resume. The angle is not the right one for her pleasure, but there's a satisfying efficiency to the rhythmic mechanics, and this efficiency is itself pleasurable. She whimpers, and he accelerates. Now she is the one shielding his head from the reverberations.

It takes a while for him to notice the oozing, but finally, he does. Something dribbles onto his bare shoulder, and he stalls. 'What the fuck.' There is a pause, then it happens.

A thick avalanche of effluvia cascades onto his back. He pauses, glances over his shoulder, flinches. He pulls his cock out of Anna, swearing. He yells at her to move, and she does, but not before the last sinew that has been holding the flood at bay gives way. An onslaught comes – a primordial plasma of rot. It smells of age and neglect and forgotten vegetables, of old tampons gathering in a bin, of silage and shit and pre-ejaculate. It descends in slops and heaps of brothy viscera — an assemblage of once-alive matter, long dead, caked to the seam of the hull's edge until shaken loose by this ménage à trois. It splatters their naked skin, coating them in death. She squeals and they dart. He bends and grabs his clothes. He dashes from the shipwreck, dancing his way into his boxers. He plants himself at a safe distance. She joins him. He swears, she blasphemes. He retches, she watches. Silence.

The walk to the tide is long and tortured — he doesn't look at her as he washes the gunk from his skin, and in one swoop the last light of the day dies. She can't get all the coagulated gunk off her shoulders or the ends of her hair, so she leaves it, not wanting to prolong anything. They remain silent as they drag sandy clothes over damp flesh, and it is not until they are both dressed and at the top of the dunes that he speaks.

'You, uh, you live just across the road, right? It's just that house there, right?' He puts a hand to his head and scrubs at the bristles she was pressing her palm against, just fifteen minutes ago. The smell lingers on both of them, is now supplemented by bracing salt. Anna turns her nose towards her clavicle, sniffs, grimaces. She nods. He nods.

'I think, uh, probably not the night for a drink, right? I need to go home and take a shower. I'll just text my mate here, he's only down the road – he'll come and get me.'

'Yeah, okay. That's grand.' A pause while he taps at his phone screen. He darts a look at her.

'But yeah, you don't need a lift or anything like that?'

'No, no, I'm good. Thanks.'

'Colm's not gonna be thrilled at having me in his car, smelling like this shit.'

'Sorry.'

'It's fine, don't worry.'

'I am sorry though.'

'It's fine.' Another pause. 'Listen, you don't have to wait, or anything. He's just replied there, so he won't be long. You can head on home.'

'You sure?'

'Yeah, no point both of us hanging about.'

'Okay.'

She takes a step towards him – not intending a hug, just wanting to close the gap between them before it is made infinite. He instinctively retreats, and she almost laughs.

'Right,' she says. 'Okay. Thanks for coming out. I'll see you another time.'

'Yeah, absolutely. Take care. And, uh, good luck with the funeral and everything.'

'Thanks. Bye.'

'Bye.'

She turns back at the entrance to the car park. He is once more hunched over his phone, abrading his other palm with his hair. She resumes walking. She takes out her phone – there's a message from Alex: Hi gorgeous, how are you doing? She stares at the screen. What would her dad think about her behaviour? She'll never know, is the thing. Something dawns. The chicken. She didn't replace the fucking post-funeral chicken. She bursts into tears. The porch light on the hill beckons her home.

Yvonne

She dozes until eight on Saturday morning – an unlikely restfulness she can only put down to having all three of her children home. The jejune comfort of the mother: the false equivalence of proximity with safety. Even amidst the groggy mist of waking up her children are there, fully realised in her mind and in need of her concern. They persist in their exigence, even while the rest of who she is convenes more slowly. She is always, unavoidably, inescapably, mother.

She has a sore shoulder. That's what arrives second – this reminder of her physical fallibility. It accompanies her to the bathroom, where she has to sit in a performance of using the toilet before any toilet-usage actually occurs. While she waits, she listens to the house. Anna is awake, no doubt already engaged in combat, be it with a stranger online, with the inadequate morality of a contemporary novel, with whatever man she loves currently, or with herself. Anna will importune anyone she can into having a fight with her, then pity herself the effort of fighting. Yvonne admires her eldest's zeal for challenging injustice – she just wonders how much of it is for the causes themselves, and how much is for the expulsion of anger.

Matthew and Gemma will sleep for at least another hour, and then Gemma will spend the rest of the day trying to conceal her hangover, while Matthew will fidget and grunt and eat an alarming amount of food, seemingly without tasting it, all while prompting a thousand worries in Yvonne's mind about his mental well-being. People who think boys are easier to rear than girls aren't paying enough attention.

She washes her tacky skin with an oily cleanser and continues to gather the vital details of her life. She is a retired oncologist, an only child, a widow. Or, not a widow. Not quite. She's an ex-widow, ex-wife to a deceased man. She owns a bockety but reliable house on Gollan Hill. There's a dog somewhere too. Yvonne should probably see to her, then a trip to Lidl for the additional bits for Monday's dinner. Then laundry, then she'll wait for her children to shape her day.

It's thankless, being a mother.
That's what her mother used to say. Regularly, often. With levity, irritation, resignation. It was the line for all seasons, the catch-all mantra for the human condition.
Her mother was a hard woman, worn down by the accident of her era. Not allowed to accept her scholarship to Queen's, expected to stay home and rear her numerous brothers instead. She became a seamstress, and by the end of her life you could tell – bad eyes and pollarded knuckles. She was a confusing, contradictory person: a product of her time and an anomaly within it. She married Yvonne's father a virgin, yet wore an apple-green dress with a matching jacket to the ceremony. She didn't want a daughter, because she knew men were superior, yet she imposed upon her rotten daughter a ruthless feminism, for the rotten daughter was expected to fulfil all her mother's thwarted desires. Yvonne needed to be excellent in the ways her mother was never allowed to be, and this expectation manifested as a ceaseless aria of disappointment, her name's two syllables recast as a demand for contrition, piped into each of their

bungalow's small rooms. Yvonne could never describe her mother as negligent, although to external perceivers it probably seemed like Yvonne was frequently forgotten about – her mother was a busy, sociable woman. She wore beautiful clothes and hosted beautiful gatherings, and to the attendees it must have looked like the child in the corner was a casualty of her mother's diffuse gregariousness, and maybe it's the case that some mothers just don't have time for their progeny. Yvonne never felt neglected, though, because her mother could sing that ode of motherly dismay as easily as she could breathe, and it wasn't until the birth of Matthew that she finally forgot how to do both. Until then, Yvonne regularly wished that her mother *was* more absent-minded, because all it might have taken was a pause between criticisms for Yvonne to muster some semblance of contentment. As it was, Yvonne was born a disappointment, and for the rest of her mother's life she was assessed on a negative marking system; she could hold steady, or she could sink, but she would never rise in her mother's estimation.

When she became pregnant with Anna at twenty-eight, her mother was not happy. Rather, Yvonne's readiness to start a family was deemed an affront to all the hard work her mother had put in, preparing Yvonne for the world by mimicking its hardness. Her mother had put on the performance of a lifetime, striving to recreate all the abrasive ways in which society parches women, and for what? For Yvonne to get pregnant this early, having barely scratched the surface of her potential? A doctor, yes, but not a notable one, and any further success would now be stymied by the straitjacket of motherhood. Not to mention, as a woman with a demanding career, her parenting would almost certainly be impoverished also. In her mother's eyes, Yvonne had committed the cardinal sin of greed, and with it, she'd abandoned standards – she'd tried to do too many things, and she would do them all poorly.

Yvonne can't even say definitively that her mother was wrong. She's made a lot of mistakes as a mother, through some cursed balance of over-correction and inheritance. She wanted to do it differently to how her mother did it, but she also couldn't fashion from herself a whole new parenting style, or a whole new mode of self-perception. Her mother's mothering was the only type she'd ever known, and though she tried to put distance between it and her own, the distance ended up negligible. For all her efforts, she was cloying where her mother had been airy and dismissive, neurotic where her mother was lukewarm, and angry — well, she was angry where her mother had been angry.

Yvonne has never thought of motherhood as thankless, because she never thought her children owed her thanks. She doesn't know if that has come across. She wishes she had done lots of things differently, but then she also finds herself thinking in the moment that she could be doing things differently. Whatever this idealised 'different' is, though, it never arrives in time. It's not so much a system of regret as a system of near-misses. She doesn't even know if she knows what the right thing is, except that it's rarely what she does. The right thing might even be for her to thank her children, for being so alive, for being so varied in their complexities. For being nothing like her, and nothing like her mother.

As for their father, he's all the way through them. Anna might think this is a quality Yvonne hates about them, but that's not true at all — it frightens her.

Buncrana is bright and already teeming — carloads of restless families pull into the An Trá Ban car park, ready to perform the pilgrimage to Swan Park. She quite fancies a walk herself; it always helps to loosen her sore hip. Instead, she follows the road round, takes the turn at Tierney's Pharmacy and parks at Lidl. She opens the boot and realises she forgot to bring the long-life carrier bags.

'Shit.' She sighs, steels herself for the chaos of the supermarket.

Being a wife, now that was thankless.

Her friends probably think that she never loved him, that he never loved her, but that's because there's a very narrow space for what is allowed to be understood as love. She doesn't mean that as some kind of tricksy, apologist stance, one that absolves people of treating one another despicably in the name of care, but just that flawed, hindered people can feel what they know to be love and nevertheless enact it poorly. She did love him, for a while, and she thinks he loved her, but they were damaged people who couldn't maintain the pretence – they'd each pretended to be something else in order to receive love, and a year into the marriage they were both too tired to keep pretending. That's something she'd tell her children, if she thought it wasn't too late to become the kind of mother who ladles out wisdom: don't try to trick someone into loving you. She doesn't think it's as simple as saying it's not real love if it's founded on a falsity, because on some level she thinks they both knew the other was putting on a show. The love wasn't a cloak, slung over a costume – it didn't tumble to the floor as soon as they revealed their true selves. It's more that they wove their love like thread, through the lattices of their imperfectly erected personas. When the lattice falls apart, the love remains, but it's stretched too thin now, with little to support it – it pulls and frays and can keep nothing out. Inevitably, other, grubbier stuff gets in.

They met at Queen's in the eighties, when she was in her third year and he was getting his PhD, publishing endless papers on microbial resistance. Yvonne lived at home and drove to university every day. She was pious and diligent and beautiful, though she didn't know it then. That's something else she'd tell her children, if she could figure out how: realise when you're beautiful and settle into it. Don't let it dictate your movements, but do allow it a reservoir in your mind, and draw from it when you need to. It's too early to tell what Gemma and Matthew look like – they're beautiful because untampered-with youth is always beautiful. Anna, though, Anna is becoming gorgeous, and even more so for how unwieldy her not yet fully developed righteousness is.

YVONNE

The undergraduate pharmacists were always objects of fun for the trainee doctors — they were dismissed as aspiring peddlers, the mindless vendors of what the medics would one day prescribe. Despite this, the two cohorts socialised together often, or as much as you could socialise in Belfast in the eighties, which wasn't much. She heard from a friend that one of the older pharmacists fancied the look of her, and she had crossed her fingers that the pharmacist in question was him, knowing he was one of the few her classmates would not mock her for. She knew about him already, because the condescension of medical students didn't negate a certain tacky competitiveness, and his reputation transcended snobbery — he was widely understood to be cleverer than anyone. She now hates how much that dictated her decision — the optics of his intelligence. That's one more thing she would tell her children — academic ability, or even raw, natural, chilling intellect, does not make someone an appropriate partner for you, and to think that it does is just a symptom of your own ego. You are not better than the love of someone less intelligent; you are not too smart for the compassion of someone stupid. Yvonne's mother had idolised *all* men, but the clever ones especially, and Yvonne carried this with her into her own romantic aspirations, alongside the confusion of not knowing whether she was superior or worthless. Folks, she'd say to her children, if you accept anything from me, accept this, my phronesis: you are neither too good, nor insufficiently good, for simple human kindness.

He was funny, and attentive. He was also gratingly ambitious, with an inexhaustible work ethic. He was fawning, but in a way that didn't feel disingenuous: he was generous with compliments about her achievements and prospects. He was indecisive, and awkward, and frighteningly melancholy. Even at the start, before she could begin to understand its source, the melancholy was there, and he never did a convincing job at hiding it — he always seemed just a little too ready to cast himself into the thick, black pit. She'd see glimpses of it, a fervour in his eyes for his own annihilation, and when she didn't hear from him for weeks at a time, she knew where he was — sitting at the pit's precipice, breathing it in.

He'd grown up in a rural unionist community, presided over by poverty and loyalist paramilitaries. His was a childhood Yvonne never quite managed to crystallise from its abstracted nightmares, even after seeing the house, even after hearing the stories, even after using the outhouse, with its horrible hole to nowhere. His adolescence was a batter, poured into a mould of violence and loss. He'd had a beautiful older sister, who caught the eye of a UVF man and was never returned. He'd had a father with a temper and a farmer's build. He was fourteen when a gun was first held to his temple, when he was first forced to hide weapons for the gang who would murder over a hundred Catholic civilians, including a pharmacist. Yvonne took these details from him, but struggled to know what to do once she had them, for how could any of this have been true? Here he was now, living in the boxy guestroom of an old woman's house in Glengormley, defrosting Iceland waffles on the radiator for sustenance. It was *funny*, his life, now: scrappy and shambolic and piecemeal. It was anecdotal, not tragic. He was poor, of course, and poorer than Yvonne – his maintenance grant alone, greater than that of anyone else she knew, was sufficient to tell her that. That said, she'd assumed that his was a simple kind of poor – its difficulties stemming purely from an absence of comfort. The poor she'd been imagining was not compatible with the barrel of a rifle, or with coercion, or with that loveless wooden shack at the bottom of the frozen and bitter field. She became scared of him, for a while, because what needed to take place in a mind to enable its proprietor to function in the wake of this kind of reality? How was he able to drive her to the cinema on Friday evenings? How was he able to sit through films that were as inadequate to what he'd endured as she was — as her entire, soft-edged life was?

He never offered the information willingly, and it was Yvonne who insisted upon seeing the place he'd come from, the place that had produced the man who for some reason had set his sights on her. Everything required aggressive siphoning, for he'd been raised in a chamber of silence. She could see the toll her needling was taking on him, even as she did it, but she couldn't stop. She needed to understand what he was, because it didn't make sense that he was so attentive to her, that he was wooing her with such determination. Their makeshift courtship was a frivolity, compared to what he'd come from — how was he not insulted to make himself so small? She thought, early on, that it must be a deception, but he never faltered, except on those days when the black of the barrel, the black of the pit, drew him away. On those days she let him be, and she didn't realise until later all the ways in which this was a deception on her part, because she has never been someone who knows how to let things be.

They were married by her twenty-fifth birthday, and she's not sure if there was a single day in which they were happy as man and wife. Marriage was the solvent that disintegrated the woven osier of their relationship, because it turned out that marriage was both too difficult and too easy – now that they'd attained conjugal legitimacy, neither felt the same pressure to keep performing, and with all the fresh challenges of building a convincing life, there simply wasn't the time to perform anyway. He turned hard and she turned brittle, and they never found their way back to softness, to pliancy. Faced with his silence, what could she do but scream into it? All she needed was a dialogue, but he had never been taught negotiation. All he needed was calm, but she had never been taught diplomacy. She yelled and he retreated. She advanced, and he barricaded himself in. They never met in the middle.

She's always found it interesting, the hold the idea of the father figure has over discussions of sex – she hates the term 'daddy issues'. Her father was wonderful. Smart and gentle and uncomplicated. He was tactile and jovial, he'd deliver hugs like mountain ranges, bestow kisses on her scalp. He died of a pulmonary embolism when Yvonne was eleven, and she spent most of the next twenty years wishing it had been her mother who had ducked out prematurely. She supposes a certain kind of unimaginative analyst might blame her marriage on the gap left behind by her wonderful, chain-smoking father, but she thinks it would be more astute to see it as a product of her mother's nastiness. She married the first person who was impressed by her, the first person to tell her she'd done well.

They discovered themselves to be unexpectedly good at creating children. Anna was a total surprise, the result of a rare moment of intimacy and a cavalier attitude to contraception, Yvonne assuming, for no reason other than it just seemed typical of her, that she was infertile. Of the ten times that they had conjugal intercourse, five were unprotected, and three yielded new people. It was the one way in which they worked the way they were supposed to – they just could never get the other parts to work well enough to make it happen more than once a year.

Before Anna arrived inside her, she'd been harangued by thoughts of leaving. She wouldn't have actually done it, she knows that – the threat of her mother's reaction was enough to stop her from pursuing the hypothetical. People like them didn't divorce, that was her mother's credo. Divorce was for the gauche, the godless, the people with too much money and too little conscience. Had her mother been given a true insight into Yvonne's marriage, her take would have been that it was in shambles at Yvonne's hand, that Yvonne was simply failing to fulfil her responsibilities.

Her mother had been an excellent wife, there was no disputing it. Yvonne's father wanted for nothing, had every friction of domesticity buffed away by her assured hand. His shirts were pressed, his tobacco was replenished. More than that, though, he was loved. Truly and solidly loved. They adored one another, and Yvonne was almost a disruptor to that, an obstacle. Her father doted on his only child, but he also did little to interrupt his wife's monologue of criticism, her swift slaps. Yvonne always wondered if, through being born, she had accidentally entered into competition with her mother for her father's attention – daughter and wife, battling it out for the finite supply of a man's affection. When he died, Yvonne's mother was officious, but ruined. She got on with things, because she was proud and composed and would sooner die than let appearances slip, but she was never happy again, not really. Gone forever was the laugh she reserved for his jokes, the wide smiles and indulgent finger wags, the nights spent swaying gently to the radio as they put the kitchen in order. All marriages, to Yvonne's mother's mind, should be made in the image of hers, and if you were performing marriage correctly, it was simply a case of hoping that death might be patient in ending things.

If Yvonne's husband had left *her* though (prior to her mother's expiry, that is) – she might have found a way to spin that. She was appalled by her own cowardice, her yearning to be made an object to which action was done. 'Leave me, please,' she would think in his direction, 'Walk away and force me to design a different life for myself.' In the eyes of her mother, it still would have been Yvonne's fault, inevitably, but the blame might have been more evenly distributed. Where was *his* staying power? He'd made his bed, after all. Didn't these country folk know about hard work?

But then there was Anna, a perfect promise and perfect obligation, the fire blanket plopped upon her agonising, pulsing on the ultrasound's watery screen. She promised herself she would revisit the question of her marriage later – for now, this was enough to be getting on with.

She laughs at her own naivety, now – the very idea that she would find the resolve to end things *after* they had raised a child together. There had been an implicit agreement that there would be no more children, that Anna was a sufficient challenge alongside all the other challenges. But then, once they'd got to grips with Anna, with the pharmacy, a stalwart on the Culmore Road, with her work, with themselves, they decided they might as well keep going. Sunk cost and all that. They moved from the slender two-bed in Kilfennan to Gollan Hill, a move motivated largely by unsolicited advice, as everyone around them extolled the benefits of buying in Donegal. The house was shabby but well built, with more space than either of them knew what to do with. They let Anna have the room downstairs, partly because she'd decided the upstairs was haunted by the ghost of a racehorse, and partly because it allowed them the tacit agreement to have separate bedrooms. Once the house was in decent shape, they decided Anna should have a sibling, so with all the specificity and allure of the shipping forecast, they summoned Gemma into being. Shortly after, Yvonne had a rare moment of giddiness, as she ferried her perfect umbel of a toddler from room to room. She realised that the streamlined order of her life, and the shining faces of her children, were worthy substitutes for romance, and she informed him that they should have one more. She ignored his lack of enthusiasm and pressed him to her will, like she always did.

Lidl is noisy with bodies. Those still shopping weave in and around the queues, and a harried man bumps into Yvonne's basket. 'Sorry,' he mutters, juggling a multipack of crisps and three 2L bottles of lemonade. Yvonne says nothing. She sidesteps to let him past.

It was during her first trimester with Matthew, when her mother was on the final stretch of her long walk to what comes next, that whatever act of masonry had thus far been sufficient to keep him out of the pit broke. He'd sold the pharmacy the year before to a huge conglomerate, for a sum never seen before by either of them, a sum Yvonne didn't realise would one day get split between them in the settlement. When the offer came through, they discussed it, with the dispassionate pragmatism that governed their better conversations, and though he expressed some concerns about not working, even temporarily, Yvonne knew the financial security was more important, and would allow her to enliven the andante meander of her own career. She said the sale would let him spend more time with Anna and Gemma, the career break would give him time to concretise his fatherhood. It was this that cinched it, for he loved his daughters with a maladroit but moving totality, one that Yvonne couldn't quite keep herself from resenting, because wasn't it just so predictable that he would get to be the fun parent? Wasn't there a rich and indomitable canon of caustic, militant mothers, and jovial, part-time fathers, for them to be inducted into? She could see what his clownishness was for – to keep his past as far away from his children as possible, and she respected him for that, and understood its necessity, but that didn't make it any easier to witness. She resented that he got to, however temporarily, outrun his shadow and become buoyant, silly Daddy, the parent who could devote hours to make-believes so narratively complex his tiny gamers couldn't even follow them half the time, the one who could give himself over, entirely, to affection. In some ways he fathered a little like Yvonne's own father had, and this observation gave her such a crisis of existentialism that she couldn't make direct eye contact with him for a week, appalled that he might have turned her into something reminiscent of her mother.

In what has become a recurring pattern of her life, she was swiftly punished for her dissatisfaction. She came to be furious at herself for ever ruing the days where he was present, because one Tuesday she woke up and he was gone, and suddenly she was four impossible things at once: a pregnant mother of two, a doctor, a daughter to a truculent, dying shrew, and the wife of gravitational collapse. In selling the pharmacy, he'd attained the financial and material safety he'd been fighting for his entire life, but now that he didn't have to focus with dogged determination on the future, there was nowhere for his thoughts to go but the past.

It happened in increments, the practical conditions of his descent, and he was never so at ease with his own suffering as to capitulate entirely – meals were still prepared and bills were still paid – but it was clear his functionality was being powered by some backup reserve of duty, which remained even while an invisible behemoth sought to drag him through the floor. Yvonne couldn't intervene, though – there was too much else happening amidst his wretched misery. Had theirs been a different kind of marriage, he might have been her priority, but they'd long ago relegated one another – they were colleagues in domesticity, associates in survival. The children came first, then her mother, then him, and the first two demanded so much that she could only tend to him as though he were a plant. She roused him from bed every morning, coaxed him towards his ministrations, then left.

Anna was delivered to school, then she and a fussy Gemma went about the business of Granny's dying.

The realisation that she might be more like her mother than she could bear to admit had stoked in her fresh sympathy for the furious woman in the hospital bed, but it was a sympathy that was hard-wrought. Her mother seemed to have decided that, because she couldn't take her cruelty with her, it all needed to be spent. Every day she told her pregnant daughter that her make-up was whorish, that pregnancy had ruined her figure, that she'd abandoned her career, once again, to become a nursing sow. She offered these decrees between thick, malignant coughs, and Yvonne hated that these painful shudders, the sign of her mother's tremendous suffering, also heralded her own respite.

Her mother's demise felt like the first thing on an impossible to-do list: get mother peacefully dispatched, get baby safely delivered, mend broken husband. Six weeks before Matthew arrived, in a rare moment of amenability, her mother complied.

Her mother's death didn't occur in the way Yvonne had expected. She thought her mother would go noisily – punctured and defeated, broken and bested. The reality was more like fiction for its serenity. She was beautiful, somehow, in her final moments. Yvonne has been reticent to ever admit this to anyone, in case she sounds like a loon – she has always despised the lazy propensity to imbue the chaos of lived experience with hokum theories of the spiritual, the transcendental, the otherworldly. It's the symptom of an unscientific mind, a gormless refusal to interact with reality as it faces you. She hates horoscopes, mystics, all hagiographic renderings of perfectly explicable phenomena. She was brought up in a solemn, Presbyterian household, where belief mattered less than good sense, respectability, modesty. Though she tried for a while to replicate the structure of weekly churchgoing with Anna, she couldn't make it stick past Anna's eighth birthday. Yvonne has always tried to see the value in it – faith – but ultimately all that church seemed to be useful for was the reminder that life should have a certain staid diligence to it, and after a while she simply didn't need any reminder of that. She'd like to believe in God, but she can't shake the suspicion that it's a cop-out, a delusion for frivolous people. The requirement of something unseen to legitimise that which is tangible feels to her an insult to life, one that absolves people of trying to live truthfully, with respect for all existence's difficulties.

That being said, there *was* a moment – just a moment – when Yvonne held her breath so as not to miss her mother's final exhalation, her last dynamic offering to the atmosphere – when something strange took place. Her mother's skin seemed to take on a light, a halation that smoothed the deep-set lines of her ancient face. Her hair, which was matte and grey and wiry, softened and paled around her widow's peak. She looked peaceful, which is itself a kind of beauty, and Yvonne was reminded of the day after her father's death, when she was summoned to the kitchen to find her mother, pink-cheeked and youthful in her furious uncertainty, standing over a table laid with a feast: a meticulously roasted chicken with yellow potatoes, their skins as taut and crispy as fibreglass; parsnips and cabbage and carrots steaming. For an hour they sat together, saying nothing, her mother habitually shredding skin from the bird's skeleton onto Yvonne's plate, and Yvonne understood that this was her mother's vocabulary of comfort – whether it was the case that she didn't trust the words, or that she lacked them completely, what Yvonne's mother did trust in was duty, and by upholding that duty, even in the face of the unimaginable, she showed her daughter that they could continue, that they would survive. When her mother died, Yvonne was cast back for a moment to that night: her mother's face bright over the vestiges of their meal. She allowed herself a second to inhabit the irrational – that her mother might be aglow with some ontological change of state – and then she gathered herself. She whispered a secret, shameful prayer to the ether, then placed a hand on her abdomen and promised the baby inside that she was here, that she had everything under control.

The whole prospect of labour appalled her. Not because of the pain – by the third time round she was half-expecting the baby to crawl out of its own volition – but rather because she knew her colleagues would insist on visiting, and how could she explain why her husband wasn't there, making inadequate jokes and wielding flowers and shepherding their pre-existing blessings? How could she explain that it wasn't his fault, that she was angry with him for being absent, yes, but not justifiably, not reasonably.

It was Amy, in the end, who performed the role of co-parent at Matthew's birth – she spent most of her time in a corridor of the Altnagelvin maternity unit, rocking an unconscious Gemma in a buggy and singing an interminable song about poo with Anna. She fielded the questions from circling registrars and well-wishing nurses, securing Yvonne some sacred privacy as she endeavoured to push. Meanwhile, he was at home, with one instruction: stay alive. Amy called him at the moment of Matthew's arrival, and then he was there, looking gaunt and ashen and like he'd stumbled over from a different ward. Yvonne handed their son to him, hoping with a cruel naivety that the baby would shock him back to life. She also wondered if she'd transferred, umbilically, some sense of the palpable chaos of her life to the baby, because Matthew's birth was indeed the easiest of the three. She couldn't understand why Matthew was so eager to come out, to enter all this misery and farrago, but she was grateful to him for it. Her tiny, wrinkled son was here, and he wanted to make things easier, he wanted to comfort her.

The greatest deception participated in by the human race, Yvonne has realised, is the myth that you will one day change into someone old enough or wise enough to handle things. Your conscious mind never undergoes some alchemical transformation from childhood to adulthood, from innocence to competence. You are always just you, and it never feels any different – the immediacy of inhabiting a mind at thirty is the same as that of fourteen, as that of fifty. The light of the sun and the light of your mind, cast out through your hungry eyes, cross paths to form perception, but the only thing that ever changes is the history that perception leaves in its wake: the things you have seen prior to whatever you are seeing right now. Sure, you can try with each passing year to draw upon that history, to try and use it to make what feels like an informed decision, but you will never feel more prepared for what's to come than you do now, than you did then.

Of course, the myth that you will one day know better is a necessary one – she will not be informing her children that they will always be clueless, because she doesn't know what she would have done with this knowledge, had someone informed her. The virtue of the deception is that you aren't made to choose life with a full awareness of how frightening it will be. There is no amor fati.

She should have predicted it, she supposes, his leaving. It was not the case that the year of his black depression was a blight upon their abiding bliss. After the antidepressants and the therapy and the return to gainful employment there was a period of serenity, but what they had was still not comparable to a good marriage. They should have separated before Anna was born, and while Yvonne might like to blame her mother for their failure to do so, the actual reason they didn't is probably much simpler: they lacked the imagination, or maybe they were both too ambitious, neither able to bear the sting of failure. What seems the most likely explanation is that as teenagers they'd both conjured an image of the life that would be their salvation, and it looked a lot like this – a marriage, a home, a family. To dismantle that image and start over would have been to admit that neither of them had known what they needed, and this would have been a different kind of defeat.

A crueller theory is that Yvonne took some pleasure in disliking him, she liked controlling the occasionally pernicious conditions of their life together, stoking the intensities with jibes and bristles. She doesn't think this interpretation can be applied mutually, because for all his faults he wasn't vindictive, not in the way she could be. Maybe a part of her liked having a person to hold accountable for all the small inadequacies of her daily life. Maybe she enjoyed having someone to blame, someone to hurt.

Becoming a mother, though, wrung that part from her. She doesn't enjoy hurting people any more, and the fact that she continues to do it, that she continues to see herself choosing the path of acrimony again and again, despite the sadness it wreaks, is enough to make her weep at night. Motherhood changes you, but not enough, it turns out. It makes you better, but it doesn't make you good.

Once Matthew was safely installed in nursery school, they gave up the ghost and decided to separate. Within nine months he'd been headhunted to join a think tank at a university in North America, and this, she thought, was also predictable, though of course she hadn't predicted it – she rarely predicts the things she thinks she should have predicted. She hates that there are decisions beyond her comprehension, developments she lacked the insight to foresee. She didn't foresee this, even though it made perfect sense: it would have been against his nature to return to clinical or community pharmacy. He'd done both, and with a punctilious efficacy. It was a necessary condition of his continued survival that he find a new goal, a new mountain to climb. She pretended to be angry, but they both knew that she wasn't, that the anger had left at the same time as the last vestiges of love. The conversation was more civil than many that had preceded it.

The vegetable aisle is replete with colours. Netted sleeves of onions nestle in a box and she ferrets a bag of carrots out from its hiding place. A child in a buggy squeals as its mother inspects avocados. Yvonne attempts a sympathetic smile.

Then Anna, their precocious, contrarian teenager, decided she wanted to go to America with him.

Anna got a terrible deal, in so many respects. She had to shoulder the weight of her parents' facsimile of happiness. Her childhood was the page upon which they wrote and crossed out and rewrote the mad Socratic dialogues of their miscommunication. She wanted for nothing, materially speaking, but she also had a mother who wouldn't relinquish control and a father who didn't know how to seize it. It made sense that she wanted to go with the parent who was newly happy, newly attentive, newly sparkly, and not the one who fussed at her like a rash, but who was also distracted by her burgeoning career and her smaller, newer, more breakable children. Anna's adolescent stresses were constantly going overlooked, and there was nothing she could do about it.

There was no question that Anna could ever have gone, but it was difficult to explain that without telling her the whole truth – that her father's health might not withstand her, that her safety might not withstand him. More civil conversations were conducted, and the party line was settled upon: 'Your school is here, your friends are here, your mummy would miss you too much.' This last part, in a roundabout way, was proven true — there wasn't a night during the first nine months of Anna's departure, years later, where Yvonne didn't sob, where she didn't curse herself for being too weak to tell her eldest daughter how much she adored her. Back then, though, it was mostly empty agitprop, designed to keep Anna at home. Anna saw through it, and wouldn't forgive her, and Yvonne was sanguine about not being forgiven. At some point she became okay with being the villain.

For all her posturing, her marriage wasn't actually thankless. He did thank her. He thanked her every day, towards the end. Even before she brought Matthew home and threw herself with gusto into fixing her husband, he thanked her — he thanked her for waking him, for telling him to eat, for bringing him ultrasounds and for encouraging him to play with his daughters. He thanked her more than she felt comfortable with, given where she'd placed him in the hierarchy of her heart. It's not the case that her marriage was thankless, but maybe, like motherhood, it should have been — maybe if you're doing it right there isn't any need for thanks, because every gesture is understood as part of what's powering the engine, which isn't kindness, or charity, or duty, but love. Maybe every time he thanked her, she was reminded that there was something inherently transactional at play, and even though for lots of their marriage she might have been in credit and he in arrears, they were both losing, because the language of currency had long replaced that of love.

And yet, didn't they both win, also? Amidst the dwindling love for each other, there was love for their children, and if the decision to make these children was also the product of a transaction, then it was a perfect one.

As usual, she buys much more than she intends to, the consequence of trying to pre-empt a thousand whims – what if Anna doesn't like cereal any more? What if Matthew wants beetroot? Then there's Amy, who drinks wine like a valley drinks rain. Three new long-life carrier bags, bulging with vegetables and biscuits and coffee and bottles and pizzas. When she deposits them in the boot, she sees that the bag straps, stretched thin by the weight of their load, have left dark red stripes across her palms, itchy and hot-feeling. She pulls the boot closed and climbs into the front seat, bracing herself for the busy roads home.

* * *

The new girlfriend was another surprise she thinks she should have been prepared for. If she'd been prepared, she might have handled it better. Maybe she could have been one of those women who bears such news with magnanimity, if she'd only been prepared for it. As it was, she found herself making more missteps in real time, without the ability to stop herself. The civility with which they'd broached the divorce, and his departure, was dispensed with — she never thought about what coming back might do to him, only that it was wrong of him to return in such a way as this, romantically attached, re-established. She decided she hated him, and she used this hate to rob him of the dignity of his history. She'd always intended to one day tell her children about what their father had come from, all the ways in which their gilded, insulated lives were a product of his determination and silence. She wonders, often, just how many children across Northern Ireland are underestimating their parents, how many parents are bearing the wounds of miscomprehension with an unflinching stoicism.

Anna knows a little, of course, but not enough. She doesn't understand the idiosyncrasies of this place. She thinks she can tar it all with the fat brush of her nascent, bleeding-heart socialism, that here is just like everywhere else. She thinks she can simply *declare* herself Irish and that's all it takes. She infantilises her daddy, thinks of him as some kind of upstart, plucky underdog, a well-meaning parvenu who drifted into a current; not someone born in the depths of the morass, forced to march constantly just to survive.

When he came back with his beautiful, new, American girlfriend, Yvonne made the mistake of thinking he'd won some protracted war between them, that he'd used her to aid in his reassembly, only to lord his new plenitude over all of them. Of course, it was never that simple, but she held fast to the dogma, spouting it at her daughters like bile, and though she hated herself for it she simply couldn't stop. And now what? What must her children possibly think, now? What can they possibly feel about this man she has insisted on keeping a stranger? In refusing his children access to the truth, she has denied them any chance of understanding. She has denied them the opportunity to mourn honestly.

And then there's the question of Sasha. What to do about Sasha, now? Where to put her in the aftermath? She was very articulate over the phone, Yvonne has to concede. She didn't snivel or bawl or assume any innate camaraderie in the face of what had occurred.

She offered to take charge of organising the funeral, and Yvonne was surprised to find herself accepting the offer, was even more surprised to find herself admitting that the job felt beyond her capabilities. Yvonne had created an image of Sasha as blithe and brash, a halogen beam showing up the dusty dilapidation of her new environs, stripping it of its complexity. Instead, she was reasoned and thoughtful, keen to accommodate Yvonne and the children in whatever way Yvonne thought best. It made Yvonne wonder if he had painted his ex-wife as a tyrant, a feudal lord in need of constant appeasement.

He left a note, is the thing. Of course he did – he wasn't selfish, or reckless. He will have wanted them all to know that, to his mind, this was the best decision. Sasha offered to bring it over, to share the hard copy, but Yvonne declined, politely – instead, she had her take a picture and send it, not quite ready to subscribe to the idea that a mutual loss was all bedfellows took. She also didn't want to have to explain to Sasha why she wouldn't be telling the children about their father's final missive right away, why her actions had led her to this cruel and baffling tantalus.

The lane up to the house rises to meet her, its surface pockmarked. She really needs to get it tarmacked at some point. The car crunches onto the driveway and she brakes, turns off the engine, exhales. The sea sleeps before her.

On Monday, she will take her three children to the funeral of their father, her ex-husband. She has got so many things wrong, and she has no idea how to feel. She wants to cry, but she hasn't earned the right, so she cleans and fusses and frets instead. She buffs away her children's fingerprints, like they are a stain on the home and not her entire reason for being.

On Monday night, after the funeral, she will tell her children everything. She will cook them a meal so hearty and nutritious it will communicate the love she so often fails to, just like her own mother did for her. She will let them read what was written in his note, and she will finally tell them who their father was.

Amy arrives at half four, with all the usual paroxysms — her squashy bags writhe on the floor like leeches. Her new fringe makes her head look like a fleur-de-lis.

'Hello gorgeous!' Always the hug like she's just returned from a war, always the greeting like she's some horrible American, always the bad joke. More recently, the stupid car, strewn across the driveway as though blown in from the coast.

'Hi Amy.' The fringe smells like chemical raspberries and smoke.

Amy is actually her cousin, not sister, though it seems pedantic to keep reminding her children of this. That anyone would mistake them for sisters is laughable – Amy fills the skin of her life like a nectarine, she is overpowering and brazen and gauche. She's from some planet where nothing lingers or turns rancid, she simply flips the grittiness of everyday resentment like it's a game of Pelmanism, then forces you to acknowledge how small your own grievances are, in a way that's almost insulting.

People who don't understand her probably find her unbearable, which isn't to say that she's not – she's arrogant, and her flippancy can come across as a vacuous, quasi-spiritualism. She certainly doesn't *not* look like someone who believes in astrology, or in the radical power of positive thinking. There's more to her, though, Yvonne has learned over the last two decades. Her joy is derived from a cynical ratiocination – it's not so much gallows humour as it is gallows happiness.

Yvonne knows that years of watching patients succumb to lung cancer and leukaemia has made her disdainful of more trivial misfortunes. It probably wasn't productive to begrudge her children their sobbing over scraped knees and broken toys, just because the scrapes didn't come with a side of engorged lymph nodes. Perspective isn't a catch-all term you should weaponise against personal suffering, and if it is, she could probably do with using it against herself from time to time, when she's caught in some agonised typhoon over a broken bowl or a dented car. This is where Amy is useful, despite her occasional wiser-than-thou-ness, because she doesn't participate in this miserable dance. She laughs off the small vicissitudes, and she manages to do so without ever uttering that ghastly, criminal word: 'perspective'.

They weren't close, growing up. Yvonne's mother kept her sister and brother-in-law, Yvonne's aunt and uncle, at arm's length, decrying them as bad and immoral and flighty – Amy's father was a lapsed Catholic, which Yvonne's mother thought an affront to all decency. 'Married to a papist,' she would spit at Yvonne in private, like it was a betrayal. Yvonne is mortified to admit she failed to recognise the full malignancy of this view until later, when similar accusations were directed at David Trimble. Reared in this environment of pompous piety, Yvonne became half-convinced her younger cousin was tainted and feral. In the long pauses between seeing her, she developed an image of a filthy little beatnik, culturally impoverished and tragically lacking in the important Presbyterian traditions of self-castigation and joylessness. Even now, Yvonne can't quite shake her inheritance, the feeling that the community from which she came was not so much a political or cultural product as it was phylogenetically determined, that the wariness she was instructed as a child to feel towards Catholic nationalists was no less optional than the bad joints and wiry curls she got from her parents.

In the end, it was Amy who corrected their historic estrangement, with that puckishness she uses to get people to do what she wants. She wrote Yvonne a letter shortly before Anna arrived, congratulating her on being a 'stylish working girl, with an impending baby to boot!' and informing Yvonne of her intention to visit. Yvonne complained to her husband for hours about the audacity of the gesture, while he nodded and wriggled in silence. She could not summon sufficient reason to prevent the visit though, and a week later a chubby-cheeked woman with tacky hoops in her ears and a ludicrous fur coat arrived at the door, looking like she could predict the next three decades of her older cousin's life, and wasn't sure if she was amused or appalled.

Yvonne was appalled by her, at first. Amy was wry and artsy and undaunted. She was complacent, and bisexual, of all things. She exhibited no doubt that she and Yvonne were destined to be lifelong friends, like it was inconceivable that Yvonne might not want her. She plunged herself into Yvonne's life as though she were a wish Yvonne had cast, freshly granted.

With hindsight, she should have known they would become close. Despite Amy's foibles, or perhaps because of them, in many ways she was exactly what Yvonne needed at that moment, amidst the chaos of her life: her mercurial marriage; her poky, hygienic house; her suppressed concerns that she'd got it all terribly, horribly wrong. What Yvonne needed was someone to talk to. Not about the baby, or the bills, or her patients' treatment plans, but about everything else, the subjects that had been left to gather dust in the attic of her imagination. She needed someone to remind her that she existed beyond the details that would one day form her obituary, and while Amy might have seemed to her a ghastly hedonist, Yvonne had become a dour priestess, worshipping at the altar of her own sense of obligation. And so, she let her in, and within days the house she shared with her monosyllabic husband felt less like a sepulchre. He got on well with Amy, and Yvonne tried not to be jealous, because she knew that disposing of Amy out of pettiness would only punish herself. For a fortnight she took relaxation for a test drive, allowing her cousin to flirt and laugh and diffuse all the tension, and for a fortnight she was able to pretend that things weren't nearly as bad as she thought.

Amy doesn't know that Yvonne has read the poems that arose from that period – the poems that ended up launching Amy's career. If you could even call them poems, that is. In Yvonne's day, poems had line breaks, and something resembling a rhyme scheme. These were just blocks of prose-looking absurdity, detailing with an infuriating, anecdotal tone a hopeless relationship. Amy no doubt thought Yvonne would take offence at the very obvious rendering, so never offered them up for inspection, but in actual fact she found them quite funny and clever, despite their immaturity. Amy's artistic ego is too big to countenance that her writing might not utterly devastate its subject, but Yvonne's ego isn't *so* ungovernable as to not endure a little skewering. Besides, romantic miseries all look much the same, provided you squint enough. Yes, it was Yvonne in the poems, but it was also countless others, and what did it matter if someone else recognised her in the words? It might be nice, even, for a stranger to hold her in their thoughts for a second – this perpetually suffering, word-made portrait of a woman.

It was Amy who told her she could get out, if she wanted – she could abandon the marriage. They were walking towards Culmore Point, Amy dressed in what she kept referring to as 'solidarity dungarees', because of Yvonne's huge belly, clad in thin cotton overalls and pressing a convex into the world as they walked. They looked ridiculous, in their half-matching outfits, like a comedy double act, or a before and after in a Weight Watchers campaign. It was a bright evening in early autumn and the Foyle was pale platinum, scattering light like confetti. They sat on a bench and gazed at the Lisahally Power Station, at the thin grey cursive of its silhouette.

'You know,' Amy started, as though about to offer one of her silly hypotheticals: how many bananas could you eat without dying? Would you eat a person if they gave you permission? Yvonne was constantly having to remind herself that Amy was barely twenty, that this was probably what all twenty-something-year-olds thought about, now that it was the nineties, now that a peace agreement felt possible and people were allowed to be whatever mad thing they wanted: aspiring writers, openly bisexual.

'What?' she said, rubbing her belly and soothing herself into the lobotomised state the game required, one where logic and responsibility and sense were dispensed with. It was when she glanced over at Amy, who continued to stare straight ahead with an uncharacteristic comma of uncertainty looping her eyebrows together, that Yvonne realised she wasn't being asked to debate the possible merits of cat milk. 'What is it?' she repeated.

'I know you think you can't, that it would be too complicated, or difficult, or "not the done thing".' She said this in what Yvonne assumed was meant to be an imitation of her mother's voice. 'But if you're not happy – if this doesn't feel right – you don't have to stay. With him, I mean. I get that it's not that simple, especially with the baby coming, but you could still do it. I would help you.'

She feels guilty now, for her reaction. Because she laughed. She laughed, and then she slapped her, and then she laughed again, with a greater ferocity. First, she stood up from the bench, with some difficulty, and she took a few steps forward, and then she turned. Amy had her hands on her thighs in a posture of seriousness, but she was dressed in denim dungarees, with her hair in thin pigtails, like a baby's hair. She wanted to be taken seriously, yet she was just a baby, adopting the mannerisms of adult conversation. Maybe this is what prompted the strange combination in Yvonne of laughter and anger. There was the small, timorous giggle, which set her lungs echoing, which was cut short by the surprise of her hand, bolting from her belly to connect with the ridge of Amy's cheekbone. There was a flat thud, and Amy's head did not twist on her neck, but instead wobbled on the horizontal, held partially in place by her shoulders, which tipped too, to one side. Then, her upper body restored itself to its upright position, and a second later she was sitting exactly as she had been, on the bench, as though nothing had happened, as though Yvonne hadn't slapped her with all the might her pregnancy-atrophied muscles could manage. They looked at each other, and then it was Amy's face that set Yvonne laughing again, because her expression was not one of shock, or pain, but grumpy indignation. It was an expression Yvonne hadn't seen before, but one she would become very familiar with later, once Anna was born, once Anna started to have those dreadful bouts of constipation that would require Yvonne to tilt her little buttocks into the air and insert a grape-sized suppository. The look of outraged ignominy, of having to endure such indignity – that would become Anna's signature expression, and it was the look on Amy's face right now, like there was some grand system governing the way of things, and even though no one had bothered to explain it to her, she was nevertheless expected to muddle along with it. That's how Amy looked, after Yvonne had slapped her, and though the slap wasn't funny, this reaction was – the Weeble-like tilt of her torso, the scowl of private dishonour – and so Yvonne could not stop herself from laughing. And this time it was not a titter, it was a fateful bellow of something primal, a call from the place deep inside the body where joy and despair meet. She laughed so desperately that urine seeped from her put-upon bladder and darkened the front of her flimsy overalls. She felt a longing for something undefined, and this longing pressed the laughter from her body. Eventually, Amy's face settled into stillness, and she stood, and she tried to wrap her slender arms around the huge suite of Yvonne's torso, and when she couldn't quite manage it, it set Yvonne off once again, and this time it set Amy off too. Soon, they were two defective spectacles, squealing before the calligraphy of the power station, into the remnants of the season's final ripe sky.

YVONNE

'Thank God you're so young,' she told Amy on the walk home, and it was this that preserved them through the moment – the idea that Amy was too young to understand, that Yvonne was too old to change the trajectory of her life.

They spend Saturday evening at the kitchen table, working through two bottles of wine. Gemma and Matthew go to their bedrooms early, to conduct in private all the secret conversations that don't matter at all and yet desperately do. Amy is more subdued than usual, but Yvonne doesn't have the energy to wheedle out whatever epistemological crisis is absenting her, that will no doubt find its way into the next indecipherable tome of poetry. Anna comes home early, like she said she would, but she doesn't answer their giddy invitations to join them when they hear the door slam, and an instant later she is upstairs, cranking the rusted dial of the shower. The boiler screams, and with it Yvonne's placid mood fades. She doesn't want it, but she can feel it descending – the cloud of malaise. The slow projector of her imagination sets rolling a thousand short films, each depicting a different moment in her life when someone she loves has dismissed her. She scowls into her wine.

'Hey,' Amy says, reaching over and poking her hand. 'What's that face about?'

'Nothing. I guess she's just in another foul mood.' She sounds like a grumbling child, she knows that.

Amy laughs, and Yvonne wants to hit her. 'Probably understandable, to be fair.'

'Not if she takes it out on me.'

'It might not be about you.'

'It's pure selfishness, though. She's not the only one grieving.'

'No, I know, but –'

'I just don't know why it's so hard for us all to be civil, for the sake of a few days.'

'Maybe you all can be, it might just require everyone giving everyone a break.'

Yvonne doesn't respond, swatting away the invitation back to serenity.

Amy tries again. 'This weekend might be a good chance, you know.'

Yvonne stiffens. 'A good chance to do what?'

'You know, loosen up a bit. It's going to be a tough day for everyone, so maybe you could let them know that it's okay to –'

'Yes, yes, it's all on *me* to be more lenient. Look, I know they all think I'm an ogre –'

YVONNE

'Nobody thinks that –'

'And I know *you* think I'm an ogre, with *bad* priorities –'

'I don't! It's just –'

'And I *know* everyone just loves to blame me, to say that everything is shit because *I'm* shit, and *I'm* unreasonable, and *I'm* a bitch –'

'Evie –'

'And it's *so* easy for you to just waltz in and tell me to loosen up, even though *you're* the one who's been in a mood all evening – don't think I haven't noticed! – but some things are worth caring about, Amy. Sometimes it's *not* unreasonable to get annoyed when you're treated like some horrible witch by your own children, and just because *you* get to saunter off to your artsy life when it suits you, it doesn't mean that my feelings aren't important! *I'm* the one who's trapped here, and my children can't stand me, and they think I don't care that he's dead, but he was *my* husband, and he left me, and now I'm constantly on eggshells in my own house, and you've *never* understood, you know, Amy. You've never respected me, and you think I'm just some old-fashioned harpy who can't mother her own children properly, but if you aren't going to help me get through the next few days, if you aren't going to help me make it through the funeral, then you should just go, because I'd *love* to see you try and deal with what I have to, with your adolescent life and –'

She's going too far, and she hates it, and she can't stop. She's spiralling, but there's nothing she can do to pull herself out of it; there is only one way to go. The frustrations of time and helplessness and futility; of children, small and broken, dying in hospital beds; of her own children, entitled and smug and so alive and thank *God* for their health and their life; her fruitless attempts to keep them happy and safe; the wreck of her marriage; the poison of this place leached permanently into his veins; the never-ending stream of fear and anger. It's all there in the spiral and she can't block it out. Her face is hot, and she feels like she might break, or break something, so she keeps talking, but the talking just draws her further into the maw of abyssal fury that's waiting to consume her, and she doesn't want to keep going, but there's nobody to help her. She's practically spitting, now, she's spitting like a monster at her best friend. She hates Amy, she hates herself.

'Yvonne. Yvonne, shut up.' And then Amy has stood, and she's rounding the table, and she's not so much hugging her as compacting her into a small, pressurised ball of primitive matter, and she just keeps repeating, 'Shut up, shut up. Stop it. Stop it, now. Listen. Stop talking, and listen.'

She shuts up, and Amy continues to squeeze her, to squeeze the hot, bilious air out of her, until there's none left for the thoughts or words to feed on. They flicker and shiver and start to fade. She feels the brattish traitor of her heart slowing down, and still Amy squeezes, uttering words with a flat, rhythmic authority: 'It's okay, you're okay. I'm here and we're fine and it's fine.' Part of her hates it, the awful condescension of it, because of course Amy would think that this is all it takes, that her thoughts are so facile as to be diffused by brainless chanting. She wriggles against the grip and tries to speak, 'No, Amy, and this is it – this is you not respecting my feelings and –' but Amy just keeps squeezing and talking, and Yvonne can't access the oxygen needed to ignite the words to interrupt her, and she feels so limp. She knows the calm is coming and she wants to resist it, because her anger is not misplaced, it's not, but the calm comes, and the spiral dwindles. Amy's hand is tugging her back from the edge and back into the kitchen. She allows her body to settle into the embrace, and she listens to Amy's words until satiation sets in, and they devolve into an ancient, shapeless comfort. When Amy asks, 'Okay?' she nods, and Amy takes her arms away.

'I'm sorry,' Yvonne says, and they have made it through the moment once more, Yvonne carried on Amy's back, the only person who knows about Yvonne's own pit, the one she has lived with her whole life, fearing the day the foundations might give way to the eroding earth.

They go back to the wine. Yvonne is embarrassed; Amy won't let her be. Yvonne tries to coerce Amy into revealing her own distractions; Amy refuses, and Yvonne pretends not to be annoyed. They talk about Amy's work instead. She shows Yvonne the first draft of a new poem she is writing, and Yvonne is startled anew at this person, at the non-job she's made a life from, at the way her mind translates the world as she encounters it into clauses and images, by turns horrible and banal and startling. When the scream of the shower stops, Yvonne takes her wine and waits by the bottom of the stairs. Anna trundles down, wrapped in a towel – she looks pristine, pink as carnations. Her mind is elsewhere, and she's startled by the ghost haunting the banister.

'Jesus!'
'Oh, sorry.'

'You scared the shit out of me!'

'I wasn't exactly hiding, Anna.'

'Still, though! Why are you lurking outside my room?'

'I was waiting for you!'

'Why? What do you need?'

'I don't *need* anything – and this is my house, by the way!' The prickling, always there, never fully extinguished. The scowl of her perfect daughter there to incite it.

'I'm well aware this is *your* house.' Her perfect daughter's fiery pugilism, always primed.

They face off. The skin on Anna's shoulder is like icing on a birthday cake. Yvonne focusses on that.

'Did you have a good night?' Her first daughter's impossibly lovely bare skin.

'It was fine.' Her first daughter's impatient suspicion of her old, sad mum.

'Thanks for not coming in too late.' Her first daughter's difficult nature.

'That's okay.' Her first daughter's fragile ego.

'Do you want to come and have a glass of wine with your aunt and me? We're going to open another bottle.' Her first daughter's unknowable days.

'Um. I'm a bit tired, actually.' Her first daughter's flinty disposition.

'Go on, sure. It's still early. Why don't you put something comfy on and come join us?' Her first daughter's blindness to her own vibrancy.

'Um. Sure. Okay. Give me a sec.' She opens the bedroom door a crack and slithers in, as though the sentinel of some hallowed treasure.

'Okay, pet.' Her first daughter's desperate need for worship. An old, sad mum's yearning to offer it.

Sunday brings calm. She changes the sheets on Matthew and Gemma's beds while they loll in the front room – Gemma scrunched up on the sofa, Matthew draped across the armchair like a spill. Anna refuses her entry to her bedroom; she says she'll change the bed sheets herself. Yvonne hands her the fresh bundle with a thanks. She's a good girl, really. Yvonne offers her children hot drinks, cold drinks, toast, snacks. Anna tells her to stop fussing, so she starts jotting down timings for all the various dishes that will need cooked come Monday evening. Amy takes the dog for a walk, so Yvonne goes through her emails and gets started on lunch. She straightens her funeral outfit on its hanger for the fourth time – black, wide-legged trousers, a pale silk blouse. She'll look like a brutalist municipal building, the stark monolith of ex-wife.

In the lull after lunch, Amy suggests an outing. Her big, wet, shining eyes rove the table, seeking acquiescence. The dog raises her moppish head in confusion, then goes back to sleep. Anna laments a full belly, Gemma staring at her with an unreadable expression. Matthew has designs on his Nintendo Switch. Amy's eyes find Yvonne.

'You really want to go out again?'

'Sure, it's a wonder day!'

Anna squints at the window, ignoring Gemma's attention. 'I think it might be raining, Amy.'

'It'll pass!'

'I need to clear up here.'

'The kids can do that, can't you kiddos?'

The 'kiddos' do an admirable job of hiding their reluctance. They comply.

They descend the steps to the road, Yvonne led by the bounce of Amy's ponytail. She's completely inappropriately dressed, clad in a long gingham dress and a pale blue jumper.

'What's funny?'

'You didn't want to borrow some clothes? I have a sports bra I can lend you.'

A strange look in response, as though Amy would sooner be seen dead than in Yvonne's ratty garments. A gracious smile replaces the look.

'No thanks, mate. I'm good in my tablecloth.'

'You look so glamorous, meanwhile I look a right state.'

'Sure, nobody's here to see us.'

'Tell that to your outfit.'

Yvonne is bemused when Amy insists upon steering her to the furthest entrance to the beach, which requires a half-mile walk along the road. Sometimes it's better just to go along with what Amy wants. As they stamp along the footpath Yvonne realises aloud that she can't remember the last time all five of them had plans to be in the house together for this long. Amy can – it was shortly after he'd returned from America with Sasha. Anna was horrible and Yvonne was miserable, and Matthew and Gemma were sweetly oblivious. Amy came to bustle around noisily and feed them lasagnas, which Yvonne remembers as being largely inedible.

'I can make us one later, if you'd like – I can nip to the shop.'

'Mmm, maybe.'

They follow the curve in the road till they reach the other turn-off for the beach. Most of it is concealed by the dune's bevelled promontories, and they do not descend at first, instead remaining on the upper, gravel-coated level and heading for the old remnants of a harbour at the beach's end. The wrack of time has made it more like a succession of angled cairns, marking the burial site of its fishing trade. The water looks supernatural in colour, the slow digestion of chemicals and matter. They climb the harbour's smaller stony ridges, bending over puddles and rock pools to look for life. The wind is mild, with a bite.

'Gem's so grown up,' Amy says.

'She needs to figure out what she's going to study.'

'Sure, there's time for that.'

'She's so focussed on the wrong things – she only cares about being popular and pretty, but she *is* popular, and she *is* pretty –'

'That's sweet.'

'– and what she should be really worried about is failing her A Levels.'

'She's obviously not going to fail.'

'Probably not, but she won't do as well as she can. She won't get into Oxbridge at this rate.'

'God forbid.'

'It is God forbid! Because she'll be the one crying when she's disappointed! And I won't be able to fix it.'

'I think she might be bisexual, you know.'

'Oh for God's sake, Amy.'

'What?'

'Not everyone is bisexual.'

'I'm not entirely sure that's the case.'

'Grow up.'

They dismount the old harbour and set off across the sand. Amy takes off her trainers and socks and digs her bare toes in, fashioning grooves and divots, leaving behind the sentence of herself in braille. Yvonne assesses the complaints in her shoulder and hip, decides to keep her shoes on.

'You'll have a bit more time, I guess, once Gem's away.'

'I always think I'll have more time, but something always comes along to fill it, doesn't it? Everyone always needs something, don't they?'

'Says the former care professional.'

'Well exactly! Haven't I given enough time to other people?'

Amy says nothing. Yvonne digs the toe of her shoe into one of Amy's sand gutters. She digs it bigger.

'I'd like to do a class, I think.'

'In what?'

'French, maybe? I'd like to get some of my French back. Or maybe Philosophy, or Poetry – something that might help me get on a bit more with your mad stuff.'

'I'm flattered you think my work might have enough philosophical heft as to need decoding.'

'Maybe it's just wishful thinking.'

Amy laughs.

'I would like to understand it a bit more, though.'

'Far be it from me to stop you. I'd go with you, if you wanted, to a class.'

'Bit basic for you, though, no?'

'I guess we'd find out. I've always suspected my work might be more intuition-based than founded in any particular tradition.'

Yvonne wonders if Amy ever feels any embarrassment at the things she comes out with.

'Maybe you'll discover what your,' she adopts a plummy tone, '"tradition" is.'

Amy ignores the joke, too caught up in herself. 'Postmodernism, maybe,' she muses. 'Whatever that is. Or post-structuralism.'

'Is that like the old woman who tried to restore the Jesus fresco?'

Amy abandons her reverie. She laughs a single laugh. 'Jesus Christ, you're really taking me down a peg today.'

Not nearly enough, Yvonne thinks. She regrets the thought. 'You don't deserve it, either,' she says.

'I don't!'

They fall into step, their multi-coloured outfits like the pH scale, sweeping the beach. Amy asks her if she'd ever think about another romantic relationship. Of course, Amy *would* think that only *she* could be happy alone.

'No.'

'Don't be so quick to dismiss it!'

'No.'

'Evie!'

Amy is the only person to call her this – it's not even a logical nickname for Yvonne, but it's a vestige of that week, twenty-six years ago, when Yvonne thought the young woman walking next to her would one day grow up, whatever that means: become more sensible, maybe? Become worse, become sadder. Amy hasn't grown up, nor has she become worse – she's always been this. Yvonne is relieved, though, that she assumed Amy too young back then to understand the world, because to take Amy seriously would be to welcome in threats to the tenets of Yvonne's existence — that silence is the surest route to safety, that classifications provide clarity, that traditions have value.

She decides to offer Amy the respect she rarely affords her. She considers the question, and over many soft and sinking steps she says nothing. Finally, she says that if she ever did want to cohabit again it would be with a woman, and Amy is immediately twenty again with her puppyish enthusiasm, so Yvonne modifies her terms.

'I haven't "gone gay", before you say anything.'

'I wasn't going to say anything, except that you *can't* say "gone gay", you philistine.'

'Okay, sorry.'

'It's fine, the Alliance of Big Queers forgives you.'

'That's gracious.'

'So, what do you mean, then?'

What does she mean? She thinks she just means that her aversion to another relationship like her marriage is so extreme that nothing even closely resembling it feels permissible. But what could be more mortifying than admitting she might feel lonely? She walks, watching each thigh oscillate in perfect concordance.

'I just wouldn't do it again like before, I mean. With a man.'

'I appreciate that.'

'I just don't know how to do it. Some people know how, I don't.'

'I know.'

'He wasn't a bad man.'

'No.'

'He wasn't a great husband.'

'That's true.'

'But then, I wasn't a great wife.'

'Also true.'

'I'd probably make an even worse lesbian.'

Amy laughs, and Yvonne wonders what he would make of this conversation, if he could hear it – his ex-wife and his bisexual former cousin-in-law, joking about Yvonne's sexuality. He'll have died thinking of her as an uptight control freak – assuming he ever thought of her at all. Maybe she'll have just become a shadow on his history, the process by which he achieved his children, nothing else. He had a new girlfriend, after all – did *she* ever nag him? Did she tell him to get his nose hair trimmed? Did she tsk under her breath every time he took a beat too long to answer her most recent, urgent question?

'What are you thinking about?' Amy prods her. She hates the question – what is *anybody* thinking about? She could say literally anything, and it wouldn't be dishonest, nobody is ever thinking just one thing. She tries to blunt her irritation.

'I wonder if' – she takes a pause to neutralise her tone – 'Sasha.' Not quite successful. 'I wonder if Sasha ever nagged him to get his nose hair trimmed.'

'*That's* what you're thinking about?'

She shrugs. 'You asked.'

Amy snorts. She doesn't have an immediate response – Yvonne feels some satisfaction at this. They move their feet in step with one another.

'I think,' Amy muses. 'The Ivy Leaguers impacted his grooming habits long before she did.' She takes a moment to stop her dress from bunching around her knees in the wind. Yvonne waits, watching the gingham pattern dance. She hadn't really been listening, and by the time Amy's words find shape in her head she's unsure if she heard correctly, or if she even understands. She decides not to question it, even though she wants to. 'What would *you* know about that?' she wants to say. She thinks Amy just says things, sometimes – anything to seem wise or canny. It's an annoying trait.

They round the coast's bend and then there's something new, something colossal and ugly on the sand. She squints, trying to translate its angles into meaning. She deciphers a small part of what was once something much bigger. She exclaims.

'Oh my God, is that part of a ship? Where did that come from?'

Amy says nothing, and Yvonne wants to shake her. They approach slowly, and Yvonne wonders aloud about the vessel's safety. Have her children been near it? Why didn't they mention it, why are they *so* atrocious at providing her with pertinent information? She could scream sometimes, at how wilfully difficult young people make things. She asks Amy did she not see it earlier, and Amy says that she didn't think it was a big deal, and Yvonne is cast back to stewing over Amy's irresponsible nature, the long skein of recklessness that lines her blood vessels. It is exactly this kind of thing that makes her want to place Amy at a distance, because how can she be so complacent about the world's risks? Nothing is controllable, and Amy's hubris will kill her one day. She says nothing.

The wind abates and everything goes still. The wreck grows in their eyeline, alienating Yvonne from the predictable landscape. Its black opening punctures the world. Comparatively small, in the face of everything, but still awful. It's the barrel of a gun, the bottomless circle in an outhouse. Amy nudges her and points towards the sea, like Yvonne is a parrot, some idiot animal that can be tricked with a cloth over her cage. She takes a deep breath – she decides to play along. She drags her eyes from the wreck and pretends to be placated. She looks towards the bright diamond, a patch of teal on the sea's lid, sparkling in the sunlight. Amy's not wrong, to be fair. It is beautiful. She lets the sight in, invites it to quiet her thoughts.

Amy's eager to get back to Yvonne's confessional, but the moment is ruined. It would be ridiculous to keep rambling on, now that they've stumbled upon the shipwreck. You can't discuss the weather in a mortuary – Yvonne knows that better than anyone. She keeps her eyes on the teal rhombus in the sea, its dazzle. Amy says they should take a holiday somewhere, that there are cheap flights all the time these days. Yvonne sighs, and nods. A holiday would be nice. She just needs to make it through the funeral. She just needs to fix things with her children. She just needs the next couple of days to go right.

Amy is blathering now, trying to remember the name of the Portuguese tarts – 'You know, the little yellow, custard ones.' Yvonne knows exactly the ones she's talking about, but she can't get the name either. Her immediate thoughts are taken up with questions of the shipwreck, of whether Matthew likes parsnips, of what order they should all shower in the morning to get to the funeral on time. It's not until hours later, when she's in bed, navigating a hospitable spot on the mattress for her sore shoulder and stubborn hip, that she remembers: it's pastéis de nata, of course. God, she hasn't had one in years. They've always unsettled her slightly, the way the dark splodge on a yellow concave lid looks like an embryo, floating.

Amy

The baristas in the café are discussing the world's problems.

'I just don't think inequality should exist, you know? Some people might say it *needs* to exist, but *I* would say that it doesn't.'

Amy isn't sure why a small coffee shop on the outskirts of Letterkenny needs three baristas. The place is empty. She flicks through a slim book with a brown cover. It's a book she first read years ago.

'According to a 2001 report, no one knows whether embryonic stem cells exist as such in human embryos in the womb – that is, whether they have a presence before they are extracted from blastocysts and placed in a new, laboratory-generated milieu. It is possible, therefore, that embryonic stem cells develop after they're derived from the inner mass of the early embryo.'

She opens her laptop and types the quote into a Word doc. On another doc, next to this one, is the tentative beginning of what she hopes will be her new poetry collection. She told her editor that she'd have a first draft finished in four months. She checks the calendar app on her phone, considering the inadequacy of its graphics – each small, uniform box designed to depict a day, as though days weren't elastic. On another Word doc, hidden behind the first two, are the words 'On Syntax', which is the title of the lecture she's supposed to be giving to the creative writing society at Trinity in a fortnight. For the last few weeks she's been trying to work out whether the report on stem cells might map onto social theories of language. The baristas debate the shelf life of a single blueberry muffin.

What if, for example, in the process of disseminating a thought, we extract it from our consciousness? And if that's the case, what if the language we then use to administer that elemental thought is akin to an embryonic stem cell? After all, we can't know if the coherence or resonances of the thought were there prior to its extraction, because our only mechanism for giving meaning to our experience of consciousness is language. What if the *meaning* is the stem cell of the thought – what if meaning develops *after* the thought's derivation from the inner mass of the mind? Is there such a thing as meaning without language? Could there be? And if all that *is* the case, if we are simply using language to try to translate what we ultimately do not understand – the experience of thought, of individual consciousness – then how is consciousness different from any unknowable phenomenon? How is consciousness different to the fathomless swells of the ocean, or the black, eigengrau eye of a cow? She clicks onto the Word doc saved as 'New book – here we fucking go again', and starts typing.

One of the baristas, a twenty-something-year-old with bright red hair, is describing Chicago as a city with a particularly visible inequality problem. Her colleague is wowed.

'I didn't know you'd been to Chicago!'

'I haven't yet.'

The baristas nod soberly.

It's funny, Amy thinks, how resistant we are to confronting just how little we understand of our own forms, our own minds and bodies. The human body might be the world, for all the unseen and foreign processes happening within it – procedures that for the most part happen seamlessly, but that can go awry without warning, suddenly and catastrophically. It's the deceptive thing about language, how it allows us to think we have control, simply because we've figured out a way to describe things, as though through sheer force of will we might eradicate all that is happening *beyond* a thing's signifier, all the stuff we don't know how to explain. That's before you even *begin* to think about how language is its own kind of wild, unfettered being, which is exactly what it is – Amy can feel its force on her laptop screen, right now, wrestling with her own designs. It's a shame, really, that language is the mode humans chose to communicate with, and that it therefore became the mode in which structures of power are cast. Imagine if dictators and statesmen had to dance their agendas, like bees. As it is, language is the engine we use to pretend that humans know more than other species, know *anything*. We use language as an excuse, not realising that our daily lexicon is one of the surest ways to say nothing at all. It's why people hate poetry, because it reveals language as strange, and not entirely ours. That tends to make people irritable. They'd sooner language existed exclusively in the form to which they're most accustomed, some neutral vessel for humanity's most tedious and evil ideologies.

That, and the fact that only a very small amount of poetry published throughout history isn't completely shit.

Imagine if everyone started accepting themselves as unknowable, every person an unpredictable rhizome, unconsciously sending out roots from blistering nodes. We're all just products of our environment, after all. No more distinct from anything as anything else. We're no more than the trees.

She normally hates writing in cafés, it's too easy to get distracted by all the encounters happening around her, but the baristas' conversation is so untethered to anything that might be mistaken for thinking that it makes for a kind of white noise. She wonders if they ever have busier service days than this. Her stupid vintage sports car is the only one on the tiny forecourt, and it's making her feel self-conscious. She got it about a year ago, trading in the Toyota with the missing back bumper and the wonky side mirrors. She's never been an especially conscientious driver – on the few occasions when Yvonne has deigned to get in the car with her, she's suggested that Amy might like to take some driving lessons as a refresher. Yvonne really can be an insufferable bore. That being said, the sky-blue paint of the little coupé is already flecked with scratches. It really does look ridiculous. It looks ridiculous in Galway, but here it's on another level, like a balloon dog in a doctor's office.

In ten minutes or so she'll pack up her book and her laptop and drive the last twenty miles to Gollan Hill. She tips her empty mug to her mouth for the fourth time. Maybe the baristas would take a break from puzzling over inequality to make her another drink. She once more contemplates the clash of the perky blue car with the piss-grey sky. The weather is performing exactly as it ought to, given the circumstances.

She forgoes the second coffee – you can't flat white your problems away. She thanks the barista triumvirate on her way out. They're discussing whether the colour blue is an objective experience, shared by all three of them.

She opens the passenger door to deposit her tote bag, forgetting about the dodgy hinge and flinging the door wide. There's a click from somewhere inside the door's mechanism, then everything ossifies. She tries to push the door closed, but it stays open, petulant, cast out from the car's body like a wing. She tries again. It refuses.

'Fuck. Fucking fuck cunting fuck.'

She puts her hands on her hips and glances around. The baristas gaze at her through the window, a roll of baking paper strung between them like they're the Fates. She breaks eye contact, looks away. She looks back. They're still there.

'Fuck this.'

The house is in full view before she turns off the main road to ascend the hill. Drivers coming from the opposite direction toot their horns at her, and she issues each one a wave or a middle finger. The house sits, solemn in the hill's lower midriff, gathering the earth tightly to its nucleus. The broken car door is winched to the car's body with the bright green bungee cord Amy keeps in the boot for exactly this purpose, having not yet found the motivation to get the door permanently fixed. The aperture between door and car permits a bracing blast of wind that whips painfully in her ear canals. Thickness noise, it's called. She doesn't mind it, really – the whole scenario is as ridiculous as it should be. She indicates to turn right, receives another honk from a bemused driver. There goes the family jester, heading home to jolly the court.

* * *

She's not sure at what point she resigned herself to this lifelong role; that of bouncing clown, the person bringing such forced levity to proceedings that nobody is allowed to settle for too long in their own ire. The conditions that required her to be like this haven't changed since she launched herself at Yvonne twenty-six years ago, and so she can't change either. Yvonne and her daughters have an unflinching knack for sniffing out truffles of bad feeling, so the trick is to overwhelm them at the first opportunity, with a joke or a song or some inanity. It's its own kind of humiliating, but that's the price everyone pays for family. To exist productively within the ecosystem you have to be willing to give something of yourself up, you need to be willing to regress or abnegate, to forgo pride or individuality to contribute to the larger whole. The problem with Yvonne and Anna is they both see the relinquishment of personal territory as catastrophic, rather than a vital concession for harmony's sake. They'd both rather die of thirst than drink from the other's glass.

It's been better in recent years, what with Anna finally extracting herself from her parents' financial teat. Before then it was all just too hard to take seriously — Anna trying to fund her independence with Yvonne's money, while Yvonne would rather use money as a leash than admit that she loves her daughter. These days, there's less to bind them together in a material sense, and with the connection rendered more fragile, neither wants to risk breaking it. That said, they also both lack the grace to declare a permanent ceasefire, so instead they go from scuffle to scuffle, calling upon Amy to intervene before either of them can actually win. That's why Amy's garish little routine is so necessary, because it allows Yvonne and Anna to each pretend that they are the magnanimous one. The only loser, in the pejorative sense, is Amy, whirling through like some mad, impotent Salome. Maybe *she's* the balloon dog.

She doesn't mind it so much, really. If it were an everyday demand she might begrudge it, but when you get to choose your moments of assimilation it's easier to approach them with enthusiasm. Her solipsism is there for the taking, the rest of the time. Thank God.

She imagines a pain in her chest, rubs it on impulse. Her damn breasts. Awful compost bags. What good have they ever done her? She catches sight of herself in the side mirror, massaging herself. Chest like Wagyu beef, face like battery chicken. Such is life.

She thinks she might be onto something, with the Trinity lecture, with the new collection — it might even be her best work yet. Jess would laugh if she heard this; she used to try and moderate Amy's demands of herself, as though ambition was a kind of moral failing. She always protested when Amy declared that every new piece of work had to be better than what had come before.

'Don't you think that puts an impossible amount of pressure on you?'

Jess never seemed to get that the pressure was the point. If you're not improving, you're stagnating. If she's just repeating herself, then she might as well cut her losses, call it a day.

During one particular rendition of this conversation, she and Jess were circling Belfast's Botanic Gardens, each gripping a coffee in one hand, the other's fingers with the other. The reflective carapace of the greenhouse was throwing sunlight, and a Ferris wheel was being erected at the furthermost point of the lawn – men in grosgrain ensembles wiped their brows and fed each other girders from a white van. It was an unseasonably warm April, and all around them students sat with bags of cans. Amy had a temporary fellowship at Queen's, her third temporary post in as many years. This is what Amy did, back then, before she got the Galway job – she moved from place to place, taking up short contracts. Jess followed her, because that is what Jess did, back then.

'But surely there's *no* body of work by anyone that demonstrates a straightforward upward trajectory. Even the best poets have a dip or a blip at some point.'

'Ah, but the point is, with the best poets, the dip or blip represents risk! They tried something daring and new, and maybe it was flawed in the execution, but the point is the *idea* was more interesting – *that's* what I mean by improving.'

'Okay, whatever you say. I'm not going to argue with you.'

'We're not arguing!'

'That's what I said.'

'No, because you saying that you're not going to argue with me suggests that *you* think we're on course for an argument, right? When *I* think we're just talking.'

'Okay, okay, I'm not –'

'You were going to say it again!'

'I wasn't!'

'Yes, you were! You were! I could see the words forming in your mouth!'

'Oh my *God*!' Jess's long arm thrown across Amy's shoulders, Amy's head pulled close to Jess's lips for a kiss.

* * *

Amy never got a PhD – she deemed the application process too belittling. This has exempted her from most permanent positions, which she's never really minded, because in many ways the gig economy has shielded her from the horrors of more stable academia – marking, funding applications, output assessments. She saw the best minds of her generation wrecked by office hours; many of her friends have gone loudly mad at the demands of universities, most of which are helmed by mercenary politicos with no artistic sensibility. Amy has floated through, briefly inhabiting warm, borrowed offices, giving readings and lectures in citrus-smelling halls. She has no security, but look at what security does to people.

Before Belfast, they'd been in Newcastle; before that, Dublin; London; York. Jess was a freelance web designer, working diligently from wherever she could set her brood of laptops. Amy had briefly tried to persuade Jess to teach her how to code, thinking it might be a new approach to language that could complexify her poetry. The problem was she wanted to be fluent before she had grasped the alphabet – the tedious minutiae of basic programming bored her, and within a couple of hours she and Jess had both decided the other was deficient in something, so the lessons were placed on permanent hiatus. Aside from this, their years of frugal roving were blissful – Amy knew how lucky she was to have found a partner who didn't need the mind-numbing trappings of a conventional life, who didn't object to upping and moving for every new opportunity. Amy lived for their daily constitutionals around each new place's green spaces, holding hands and bickering about free will or Sarah Lucas or Amy's artistic essentialism. Together, they devoted hours to the swans in South Norwood, decapitated by the lake's surface; they finished a hundred cryptic crosswords by the Tyne and got day drunk with the garrulous ducks on St Stephen's Green. They didn't own a house, but why would they need to? They became experts in peripatetic living, all of their books and prints ready to box and ship to wherever they went next. They had a network of friends to direct them to each new city's realm of safety, and within it they'd find perfect places to sit and read and drink and walk. Wherever one of them was, there was the other. They were thirty-five and delirious, and the frequent redesign of their immediate reality kept them energised and observant. Amy felt in sync with the part of herself that others had labelled immaturity, but that she'd always known was just a disregard for typical material concerns. She didn't crave stability, because she didn't need it – she and Jess had found a way to live that was flighty but serious, made so by the strength of their devotion to one another. She came to suspect that all the arbitrary benchmarks people use to define their lives were just substitutes for true intimacy, or creative expression. She and Jess were each other's stability, which freed them up to chase any notion, idea, impulse. The world was theirs for the taking.

When scheduling permitted, she'd take Jess to Gollan Hill, where she was immediately worshipped by Yvonne for her serene and analytical mind, and by the kiddies for her competitive approach to beach sports. Had Amy's own love for Jess not been so incorruptible, her popularity with the family might have turned Amy's stomach. These days, Amy tries to limit her visits to Gollan Hill to Christmas and Yvonne's birthday, because whenever she's there she's reminded of the indentations Jess left. Jess threw herself with an unexpected enthusiasm into Gemma and Matthew's world, and at the time Amy assumed it was a testament to Jess's understanding of community, of knowing what was needed to keep the centre held. She'd diagnosed Jess's agreeableness as an act of placation, and after these visits they'd return to their perfect, two-person harmony, free and available for whatever piece of the world might call to them next.

And then Jess said she wanted a baby of her own, and Amy realised their world was neither so permanent, nor so immune to convention, as she had once thought.

The winding road to the house is a haphazard mixture of tarmac and gravel. She's always surprised that Yvonne hasn't insisted on having the whole thing resurfaced. The little sports car tilts over a pothole and the jacked door bounces, the bungee cord releasing a low-pitched twang. Her tote bag slides into the front passenger footwell with a thump, and Amy yelps along with the car's mismanaged symphony. She pulls up onto the driveway, sliding at an awkward angle behind Yvonne's sensible and spacious Citroën. She pulls the sun visor down and opens the mirror to check her fringe. The fringe is new, and it was a mistake, because she has a cow's lick at her hairline. It means she shouldn't have a fringe, because the fringe will always sit at two different altitudes, unless she spends time wetting and flattening and ironing it down, which she occasionally does with a disproportionate resentment. She shouldn't have got a fringe, but she also hates the idea that personal style can be sanctioned. The fringe looks terrible, but maybe that's a good thing, because who cares? Hair grows, even after you're dead.

She smiles, and the wrinkles around her eyes present themselves. She doesn't mind them as much as she minds the lines across her forehead, which at least are now half-concealed by half of her stupid, regrettable fringe.

She hasn't objected to ageing as much as thought she might. She doesn't look like she's nearing fifty, which is comforting, given that she feels about thirty-one. The dissonance between her thoughts and the look of the face housing them is considerable, but not unbearable. More disconcerting is the gulf between the daily ministrations of her middle age and those of her youth, because what revolution took place to bring her to this moment, checking her emails on her iPhone, wearing a pride flag on her coat, slipping over and around the border in her gaudy chariot? How does now align with the memories of her Magherafelt childhood? Like her gentle father, liked in their community yet confined to the house like a dog on Orange march days, blanked by Kevin Henderson next door, even though the week before they'd barbecued a pig's worth of sausages together. How does now compare to the horrible RUC men, boarding the buses on the Aughrim Road? What of those days? *Listen to the rain spit in new ashes.*

Trying to explain the stains this place leaves is a thwarted mission. You are either met by redundancy – wasting the words on someone already too familiar with them – or by disconsolation, the blank look of someone for whom the terms will always mean nothing.

She takes her overfilled hold-alls from the boot – each one khaki-green, like a stuffed vine leaf. At the front door she takes a breath, readies herself for the maelstrom. She rings the bell.

When she was twenty-three, she was included in an anthology of new British and Irish poetry, and it changed the course of her life. It was the first time her writing had received formal acknowledgement, beyond the occasional poem in a journal. The work was a series of prose poems, detailing a series of encounters between a deeply unhappy woman and a misanthropic duck. The duck would rely on complicated philosophical sophistry to trick the woman into submitting to her own domestic misery over and over again, and though the scenarios changed – the kitchen table, a nice restaurant – the conclusion never did. The woman would assume the mantle of the duck's judgements, then use them as an excuse to embrace her own unhappiness.

The editors of the anthology praised the work's wit and psychological incisiveness, declaring in the anthology's introduction that the duck as a symbol imbued a bathos that made the poems all the more cutting as an exploration of everyday misogyny. The complicated thing about this take, Amy thought at the time, was that the duck *was* a villain, obviously, and not a very nuanced one at that, but wasn't the woman a kind of villain too? Wasn't it a crime of its own to be so devoted to your own martyrdom?

Amy never showed Yvonne the poems, and it wasn't until she won a prize of considerable renown, seven years later, that Yvonne began to take her seriously as an artist (or as seriously as Yvonne takes *any* artists). By then, the duck poems felt to Amy like juvenilia, so she consigned them to history. It was for the best, probably – Amy didn't think Yvonne would appreciate seeing a thinly veiled rendering of herself in something as silly as a prose poem, being condescended to by something as silly as an anthropomorphic mallard.

She appreciates now, in a way she didn't when she was twenty-three, that it's all a bit more complicated than it seems, but she also thinks it still might not be *that* complicated. In many ways Yvonne was dealt a terrible hand, but can that possibly excuse the rampant agony that finds its way into even the most innocuous dealings of her day-to-day life? Amy wonders if it's an oncologist thing, if a life spent trying to wrench people from death with professional stoicism means all the suppressed terror has to go somewhere, and where it has gone is food shopping and car tax and marriage. Or maybe Yvonne chose a life of medical servitude precisely *because* it gave her a good excuse to bring a joyless intensity to every decision.

As for the poems, they granted Amy the confirmation that she wasn't cut from where she'd come from. Her parents, though undeniably brave at one point in time, remained stuck in that point, incapable of adapting to the questions posed by their unlikely daughter. A mixed marriage was one thing, a same-sex relationship was another. She grew to hate Magherafelt, the myriad indignities her parents expected her to acquiesce to without protest.

Amy doesn't think of herself as better than Yvonne. She's not *better* than anyone. She just has a healthier approach to thinking about things than Yvonne does. The door unlocks, then opens. Amy beams.

'Morning!'

A rare look of confusion. 'It's the middle of the afternoon.'

'Mourning with a "u".'

A perceptible flinch, an audible sigh, a forced recovery. 'Hi Amy. Nice to see you.' She shuts the door like a pallbearer might. Amy dials her energy up, scrabbling in her tote bag.

'Can I borrow a screwdriver, Evie? The car door is fucked again. Also, I brought you this.' She presents the wine with a flourish.

'Why don't you just pay a mechanic to fix the door permanently?'

'Because doing something over and over again and accepting the same result is the definition of sanity.' The first small standoff. Amy grins. Yvonne rolls her eyes but doesn't push it. Amy clinks her nails on the bottle. 'Shall we have a glass?'

'Don't you want to get the car sorted first? And your clothes will be wrinkling horribly in those bags.'

'Right you are.' She doesn't resist. A victory each. She hands the bottle to Yvonne and regathers her bags. She avoids her fringe in the mirror. Yvonne doesn't mention it, though Amy can tell she has thoughts. Her expression is tortured. Amy smiles.

'What's wrong?'

'I'm afraid you're in the study.'

'Why would you be *afraid* of that?'

A sigh heard the world over. 'You know what I mean.'

'I like the study.'

'The last couple of times you've been in Gemma's room.'

'Right, but it might be reasonable of me to assume that Gemma is in Gemma's room.'

'Well, no, because the last time I put Gemma in Anna's room.'

'Which is where Anna is, presumably.'

'Yes, but Anna wasn't here last time.'

'This is all *riveting* stuff, Eve.'

A puff. 'I'm just wondering if I should have put Anna in the study and you in a proper bedroom. Except,' a flap of the hands, 'Anna would probably be difficult about it.'

'The study is fine, stop fretting.'

'Is the futon not a bit uncomfortable?'

'The futon is wonderful.'

'I'll ask the kids if they'll move.'

'I think we might all go literally mad if you do that. Please don't change anything.'

'Right, okay.'

'Go have a glass of wine, I'll be back shortly.'

'I need to finish clearing the airers.'

'Whatever gets you there.'

The study is smaller than the other rooms in the house, but otherwise it's nicer than most places she's lived in over the course of her adult life. After she and Jess broke up, she lived in Beth and Theresa's spare room in East London for a few months, and it was maybe the worst place for her mindset at the time, feeling, as she did, like the most useless flavour of ephemera, ungainly and unwanted. Curled up on the smaller-than-single bed, her eye line was dominated by items with no natural home — a vandalised guitar without strings; a horrible, half-finished portrait of Pablo Neruda; a three-legged end table; two Furbies. She gazed into the glazed, half-lidded eye of a monster (Furby, not Neruda), and felt an appalling kinship. The room smelled of jute and sweat and attic, and every night she pointed a tiny reading light at the yellowing pages of Sharon Olds' *Stag's Leap* and tried to hurry the hopelessness of her grief towards poetry, towards something worthwhile.

By comparison, Yvonne's study is a haven. The pale cream bed linen on the puffy futon looks like it's been ironed — Yvonne's neurosis once more Amy's gain. The walls are papered in milky gold and the desk is one of those mahogany, antique affairs, topped with a rectangle of bottle-green leather. There are too many copies of Amy's books on the shelves, arranged around framed pictures of the kids. There's even one of Amy, taken at her last launch. She's holding a bouquet of flowers and smiling drunkenly at the camera. That was a strange night, because the book was about Jess – in so much as anything she writes is cohesively 'about' anything – but Jess wasn't there. Because in that sense it had felt elegiac, Amy had written elegy. The book won an award that took her to Melbourne for a month, and while she was there she met a groovy priest who worked at a Jesuit boys' college, and who allowed her to annoy him most nights with the kind of questions she'd once annoyed Jess with.

'So, given humans have chosen a life of chronic species loneliness for themselves, how do you think *animals* conceive of how different species of animals experience consciousness?'

'Do you think the first law of thermodynamics applies in any meaningful way to how we think about the persistence of the soul after death?'

'Would the concept of heteronormative monogamy retain any importance if the familiar systems of society collapsed?'

Father Spinola approached these wine-fuelled inquisitions with a bemused thoughtfulness, his answers born of polymathic intelligence complexified by his faith. It was a thrilling combination, and not one Amy had encountered before – the religious types she'd grown up among had made an art of provincial, incurious tribalism. It was religion as shorthand for identity, a means of marking yourself as superior to those different from you. They knew what they knew, which was that the Pope was the devil, and the gays were responsible for the high street flooding. Meanwhile, poets, for all their spurious mysticism, tend to be deeply cynical. It was just as well Spinola was a priest, because otherwise she might have tried to shag him.

She strokes the teal, pristine spines of her books, then turns and kicks the khaki sausages under Yvonne's desk, not bothering to open or unpack them.

'That'll do,' she mutters.

She meets Matthew on the landing, emerging nervously from the toilet. What can this child possibly have to be so twitchy about?

'Hello, mate,' she says. She opens her arms and he dutifully steps into them. His hair smells like straw and cotton. 'You doing okay?' she asks his scalp. He nods, gives her nothing. She releases him, and now he asks how she is. He fidgets with his hands – the question is impulse, not a question at all. He's so polite and monosyllabic that it concerns and bores her in equal measure.

'I'm all right, thanks mate. I just want to make sure you're all coping with things okay. Want to come downstairs and hang out with your mum and me? I brought wine, but I'm sure we can find something for you – tea or ichor or MyWadi or something.'

It's so weak an invitation that she's embarrassed for both of them. He gives her a half-smile, and she feels a rush of sympathy – it can't be easy, trying to navigate his emotions in a house full of feral women. He tells her he's in the middle of a game.

'No problem. Anything especially nail-biting?'

He says no. God, it's like pulling teeth. She strokes his glossy head like he's a collie and sends him on his way, not wishing to prolong the agony for either of them. She needs a drink. She'll need several, in fact, if she's going to make it as far as the funeral.

She liked him a lot. Yvonne's husband, that is. The kids' dad. Her...whatever. She liked him. Possibly too much. There was a long period where she wasn't allowed to say it, and she probably wouldn't risk it now, even though he's dead, even though he and Yvonne were separated for over a decade and were an obviously moribund affair long before that. She did like him, though. It was funny that Amy's work found its way to rendering Yvonne, but never him, but then in many ways he defied rendering. He was nothing like the misanthropic duck of the prose poems, and maybe it's for that reason that Amy's twenty-three-year-old self couldn't resist writing her cousin into a more familiar narrative, because why was it that Yvonne capitulated so readily to the role of miserable hausfrau, when her husband was nothing like the hausfrau's typical opposite? It fascinated Amy, made her wonder if heterosexuality is doomed to repeat in perpetuity its historic failures, despite its participants' best intentions.

It's true that he was no kind of husband – that's not even up for debate, but he was decent and funny and deeply strange, in a way she wishes more people were. Some men might have blanched at being newly saddled with an unsolicited twenty-two-year-old cousin, but he never seemed to think it out of the ordinary. Nor did he seem to mind that it was her duty to side with Yvonne on all things; he accepted it as de jure, but with no obvious bitterness. She's not sure his brain was wired to think about his own ego, because he just didn't seem to have the same predispositions as other people. The problem was he pretended to, at the beginning – he made Yvonne think he was a certain kind of way, the way she'd been taught to expect of a husband, and while his lack of susceptibility to typically performed masculinity made him easy-going and agreeable, it also made him slippery and indifferent, because it seemed like he had no stake in the game of their marriage, no horse in the race. He didn't care in the ways Yvonne needed him to, and Yvonne interpreted this ambivalence as a comment upon her own inadequacy, because Yvonne was taught by her mother to interpret *everything* as a comment upon her own inadequacy. Amy saw it play out, over and over again – Yvonne's desperation to please turning to anger when it wasn't acknowledged; his mildness shifting to complete emotional shutdown.

He probably had to lie, though, at the beginning. Social mobility in the North has never just been a question of cash. He'll have known that he needed to lie to fit in, to assimilate, to escape where he'd come from. Rarely is that which is declared 'natural' *actually* natural, and that's half the problem.

Take the idea of 'nature'. The etymology of 'nature' is myriad – it contains within it ideas of the body's processing powers, its restorative abilities and its growth, but the word also evokes ideas of that which is axiomatic, something inevitable and from birth. It also, conflictingly, harbours ideas of the material world *beyond* human civilisation, and what can that even mean, in practice? What exists beyond humanity to a human eye? Even if we thought we'd encountered something beyond human influence, we'd probably be mistaken. 'Nature' as an idea has become a weapon, falsely promoting some fundamental truth beyond the body politic, used against those who aren't easily accommodated. This is how language gets declawed and then clawed again – cut away to a single interpretation that is used to hurt those who are aberrant to the created order.

You don't come from a place like this without learning what language can be made to do in spite of itself. Every question hides another; every answer betrays you in some way.

The last time she saw him was in a bar in Ithaca, New York. They sat opposite one another at a pine table next to an exposed stone wall. She'd been invited to do a series of readings at East Coast universities, and because she knew the resulting conversation would be both lengthy and fruitless she decided not to tell Yvonne that she was going to meet him. He'd been living in the States for years at that point, and for the first half hour she couldn't shake the idea that he was method-acting. He'd always had the raw components of handsomeness, but now it was like someone had filled his flesh with new history, his mouth with new dialogue. They spoke about work, about politics, about relationships – she was still in a tailspin about Jess, he'd been invited to dinner by a woman named Sasha. After several pints, he told Amy that she reminded him of his sister – the one he'd finally managed to track down, decades later, broken and bruised and dying of liver failure. It was the first time he'd ever volunteered details of his past to her, and when he spoke of their lives now, about how much things had, and hadn't, changed since they were young, he used the word 'peace' with a certain archness. He said he'd heard the word so many times that it had gone back to meaning nothing. She's thought about that a lot since, about how words start out meaningless and are ascribed meaning, but can always revert to their shapeless origins through overuse. They spoke about 'meaning', about what that word *means*, about what 'matters', truly. She told him that a fourteenth-century use of the word 'meaning' was 'an act of remembering', and they agreed that this usage was better consigned to history: in that moment, neither of them much liked the idea that meaning might come from clinging to the past. With hindsight, perhaps it was this, or maybe it was the beer, or maybe it was simply their overuse of the word that caused 'meaning' to steadily lose purchase in Amy's mind, allowing her to reach across and put her hand on her cousin's former husband's knee.

She's halfway down the stairs when she hears a clatter from the kitchen, followed by, '*Shite.*' She should have brought more wine.

She wakes the next morning to Buoy licking her toes. The study door is open, and her sleep mask has slid up and under her bad new fringe. She squints into the glow of the porous curtains, then checks her phone. This time tomorrow they'll be en route to the crematorium.

The three of them went to bed at about one, drunk and trying to suppress giggles as they embraced outside Anna's room. It was a successful evening, by all accounts. Anna had clearly had some kind of ghastly encounter that she refused to talk about – she was sullen and restless till the second glass of wine hit – but Amy was able to steer Yvonne away from badgering her into an argument. They spoke about nothing of consequence, the best way to avoid a quarrel. Obviously, they should have taken this unprecedented moment of calm to speak about the funeral – about him – but while Anna was in the toilet Yvonne issued a hushed directive over their wine glasses not to bring it up. Why talking to your children about their father needs to be scheduled in like an MOT, Amy has no idea, but she didn't argue – she has enough to think about.

She doesn't move for a second, giving in to the muscular agility of Buoy's tongue lapping at her feet in a steady rhythm. What does this elderly dog think about being alive? She pulls her heavy body from prone, leaning her back against the study wall. Buoy mounts the futon and stands on her shins, wagging her tail and panting. Amy has never much understood the pet thing, but she loves Buoy's furry little snout, the waxy black nose with its omniscient sense of smell. She loves Buoy's shiny eyes, glistening with something recognisable as hopefulness.

'Fancy a walk, Boo?' The fluffy crosier of a tail fans the room around them.

'Okay, Boo, we'll go for a walk.' The maintenance of the reef.

It doesn't take her long to notice the strange, angular shadow protruding among those of the less uniform rocks.

'What's that, Boo?' A corner this precise rarely occurs by accident. They wobble down the dunes.

On the beach, Buoy begins to strain at the harness, desperate to investigate the wreck. The stench is strong, even to a human nose. Walked by the dog, Amy is led to the husk, and even in the morning light its contents are a cosmic, impossible black – it sits by the rocks like a portal to another world. Amy collects herself in time to stop Buoy from pulling her into the wreck's opening. Instead, she insists on a nonchalant perimeter of the exterior. Its grey hide is streaked with tracks of black and green, while a lighter black than that of its interior congregates around the bars and bolts that line the wreck's seams. It's a hell of a thing.

'What's gone on here, Boo?' If anyone knows, it's Buoy. Shame that even a second spent experiencing Buoy's mind would leave her a gibbering lunatic for the rest of her life. She reaches out to touch the metal, and it's cold, like she thought it would be, but not as hard as she was expecting. There's a near-imperceptible elasticity to the metal, as though it's been squashed and kneaded by the immense pressures of the sea.

Buoy sniffs their way back to the entrance, and Amy shines her phone torch inside. The metal is the same colour on the inside as the out, but almost entirely coated in organic shades. She goes closer, wrapping the leash tight around her hand to keep Buoy close. She holds the light up to inspect; patches of bone-white and grey and green and black matter occupy the corners, spreading across the hull's insides like a rash. She takes a step inside and hears a visceral squelch – she points the torch at her feet and sees crusting sputum spreading up the sides of her rubber boots. Keeping her feet in one spot, she pivots and takes in more of the wreck's insides: on the wall opposite a dense black bitumen has gathered in folds around the floor.

'Jesus.'

She uses the torch to guide her steps, dancing along bare patches of metal. Buoy is taking a history of every lump of rotting salt, and Amy gives the leash an occasional tug to stop her from burying her face too deeply in any one globule.

There's something bright among the black mulch. She leans closer with her phone, then uses the pointed toe of her boot to unearth the bright from the black. She bends forward to look at it – it's a woman's sock. Formerly pale pink, with a sparkly trim in metallic thread. Much of the fabric is now a dank grey, and ruined, but the trim remains gaudy, too synthetic to absorb the seeping effluvia of whatever death seems to have happened here. It looks like something devoured a person, then coughed up this single sock. She kicks it back onto the tumulus of rot. It curls like a guppy.

She had other partners, before Jess, and several after, but they didn't core her in the same way. Before Jess, she'd felt with certainty that her romantic life was destined to be ludicrous, that she was just a silly girl, acting up. The lexicon of sexual fluidity had not made its way to Magherafelt in time for Amy's puberty, so she was stuck. There was no 'bisexuality', and so Amy was trapped between her incompatible desires, capable of neither righteous resistance nor easy conformity. It wasn't until she moved to Norwich in the nineties that she learned there was a word for what she was, and while this word offered her a new beginning, it also further muddied her in her parents' perceptions. Mum and Dad, for all their countercultural bravado, couldn't see their way to understanding why she didn't simply find a nice man, get married, live peacefully. They'd met in the Clark & Sons linen mill in the sixties – she was a winder, he a joiner – and their courtship and marriage were beset by hostility from all sides. They didn't want this for Amy, and so their worry became the rod they used to beat her with. Their enquiries weren't hostile, per se, but this made them more dangerous – their barbs were small enough that they could pass through Amy's pores, en masse, to sit in weighty deposits beneath her skin. They didn't yell or gnash or make ultimatums, they just wore her down with constant 'we don't understand why's. Gay, though difficult, and frightening, made sense to them – gay was immutable and fixed. Bisexuality, on the other hand, struck them as a wilful commitment to a life of contrarianism. They thought bisexuality was straightness that hadn't been finished correctly, like a skirting board extending too far over the door jamb. They'd ask her what she thought of actors on television, did she not prefer the handsome man to the beautiful woman; they told haunted tales of disease, shooting cautious glances at her body. Newly liberated with self-knowledge, she was also now burdened with the possibility of her own perverseness. She came home from Norwich less and less frequently, and away from her parents' pursed lips she went from being fearful and anxious to approaching intimacy in the way Buoy approaches each new outcrop of olfactory pleasure – with rampant caprice.

* * *

Away from home, she promised herself that she would never become the people she'd grown up among — small-minded and hateful and traditional, set on spawning more of themselves so they might pass on their bile. On her master's course, she'd been lucky enough to find people who understood, who got it. She went with friends to underground lectures on Section 28, trauma-bonded over merlot and cigarettes in dirty kitchenettes. She got a job in a bookies, and when things were quiet she read and re-read *The Remains of the Day* and *Questions of Travel*. She began to grapple seriously with questions of the suppressed and refracted self, and she'd hold court in a corner of Ritzy's on Friday nights, yelling about *Giovanni's Room*. Once she realised that people could and would be in love with her, she started thinking seriously about who *she* might like to love, and as long as the answer to that question remained elusive, she saw no reason not to try everything. After all, look at where moderation had taken her cousin. And so there was Geoffrey, a lanky and obnoxious playwright, and then Beth, a novelist. There was Beth several times, on and off again, and then Jane, who went on to become a Classics professor at Oxford, and Theresa, who ended up married to Beth. Then there was the truly special period when she became the shiny young consort of one of British poetry's ageing maestros, who did a reading at the university in early December and delighted her for hours in the pub afterwards, giving off about Marjorie Perloff. They dated for nearly a year, and during that time he bought her jewellery and took her for candlelit meals in Covent Garden. They'd sit in his enormous house in Whitechapel with port and biscuits – him toiling away at another lengthy epiphany poem about roadkill and grey hair, while she curled in an armchair with his signed copy of *The Changing Light at Sandover*. They never spoke of love, but he kissed her in a heartfelt way every time she left to go back to Norwich. He introduced her to his identical friends, all of whom were thrilled by their own tolerance of this pretty, queer 'Child of the Troubles'. They asked her about the Agreement, and she found herself speaking in authoritative, imperious abstractions, desperate to impress the aristocrats and intellectualise herself away from the place she was made. She hated herself for how she spoke about it, like she was somehow above it all, and she hated even more how they responded. They were always too rapt, too fascinated, too agog – it was as though she were describing some far-flung, foreign fantasy of war, somewhere that had no pertinence to their lives at all. She thought about telling them that they were the problem — that their greedy ideologies of empire were to blame for everything she was describing — but then they'd applaud her articulacy and buy her another drink, and she couldn't help but bask in their pandering. She felt completely beholden to this specific genre of man: old and self-assured and objectionable; sexist, but avuncular with it; rich.

She and the poet parted ways just before her twenty-fifth birthday, when his prostate started to feel 'a touch squiffy' and he decided it would be best to go back to his wife. His next collection made several references to 'the Ptolemaic spheres of the bright poet's breasts', and when anyone doubted that Amy's were the breasts in question she simply retrieved the copy he'd sent her, inscribed with the words, 'To my dear Amy, the wild daughter of Sappho and St Brigid.'

After him, there was everyone she could want, and though she couldn't quite see her way to loving any of them, she felt smart and ironical and tender in her performance of attachment.

She met Jess at a birthday party in Glasgow when she was twenty-nine, and that was that. She didn't want to be so clichéd as to be besotted with someone, but she couldn't help it. Jess was beautiful, with dark brows and huge, brown eyes. It was clear she was trying to keep her charisma a secret, but Amy rooted it out, and they spent all night swigging from various bottles of cheap pinot, squashed together on a hungry sofa. At long last, Amy had stumbled across the person from her imagination, the one who spoke to her in nimble, witty phrases – the person with a changeable face but an unwavering ability to tease her into submission. They walked home from the party at 6 a.m., the sun rising behind the redbrick fingers of Kelvingrove.

Within a year, Amy's life had a new timbre of purpose, because it no longer felt like she was trying on intensity for size. A seam of contentment ran through the fabric of her days. She felt assertive rather than bolshy, confident rather than posturing, intentional rather than scattered. She went to bed every night with a body she understood, and she slept soundly in the clammy perfection of their tessellating forms.

'Morning, darling.'

'Morning, gorgeous.'

Jess would always wake first, to start work. She'd slide out of Amy's grip and pad to the kitchen, where she'd make coffee. She always set a cup on the bedside table for Amy, who would remain asleep for another hour and then chug the cold liquid in one go upon waking. They'd find excuses throughout the day to return to bed, the bed they took apart and put together again every time they went somewhere new.

When she sees Anna and Gemma checking their phones and frowning at the blank screens, she wants to warn them: sample everything, protect yourself from the destruction a single loss can bring. She doesn't want to seem bitter; she just wishes it had occurred to her that Jess might one day leave, and she doesn't want either of her nieces to be as blindsided and broken as she was. She's found a different kind of contentment now, but it took until her mid-forties to feel confident that her life was not just one big trick her mind had played on her, that it wasn't going to pull back a curtain at some point to reveal a table piled high with unanticipated and thwarted desires. The foundational philosophy of neoliberalism is such a melancholy joke for exactly this reason, because how can there be any legitimacy to the idea of self-interest, when you simply can't predict what your interests might become? Anybody who thinks they know their own mind is kidding themselves – the mind is an animal, curled in a machine. She read an article a while ago about how oil droplets have been discovered to mimic the processes and behaviours of early life, and she liked that the word 'mimic' was used – it suggested the oil was a phoney, playing at being alive, when the more obvious conclusion is that human life itself is no more plotted or purposeful than oil under a microscope.

Up until her forty-fifth birthday, she repeatedly tried to force herself towards some kind of reckoning. She read everything she could about pregnancy, and IVF, and embryonic plantation. Sperm donation, surrogacy, motherhood. If hanging out with her nieces and nephew – if watching bumbling, bright-eyed children in the park – didn't awaken any belated yearning, then maybe the philosophical, scientific intrigue of the enterprise might, because *what* could be more mysterious and fascinating than the formation of life? What could intrigue more than the chance to witness a consciousness assembling without reason?

The perverse thing about this scheme was she started it when she was thirty-eight, at which point she and Jess had already been apart for nearly two years and it was all too late. That she hadn't brought the same curiosity to the question of children when she and Jess were trying to navigate this insoluble obstacle was typical of her long-held contrarianism. When their relationship was dissolving, most of her energy went towards anger, towards a profound feeling of unjustness, because why wasn't *she* enough? Why couldn't she be Jess's baby, and Jess hers? She didn't understand it, and so, later, when the anger had settled and Jess was gone, when all she had left was confusion, she finally did try to understand, and it turned out that, even when she *did* understand it, she still didn't want it. It was then that she was finally able to exhale.

It was in the midst of this rampant scrabbling that she'd gone to the States and met him in a cosy bar on East Seneca Street. He bought all the drinks, and after every pint he was cautious, waiting for her to suggest another, which she found herself doing, again and again. When the barman called last orders, she realised she didn't want to go back to her hotel, and when she woke up at his the next morning, she realised she wasn't ready to write the whole thing off as a drunken, self-serving blunder. He had a colleague's leaving drinks that evening, and she found herself promising to swing by after her reading. Armed with a filmy Guinness in a room full of American academics, she watched him closely in his new milieu: his hands clasped like a butler as he listened to a diatribe against leaf blowers; the impenetrable in-jokes he shared with a burly Bostonian named Tad, whose Nebuchadnezzar-esque beard danced like a windsock with every guffaw. He seemed happy, she thought, but skittish. He was an oil droplet, quivering – incapable of complete assimilation, always at one layer's remove. At the end of the night she walked him home, and as they looked at one another across the threshold, neither quite found the language to justify, or explain.

She's not sure what it was that made so much sense about the three nights they spent together. Maybe it was her appetite for recklessness, she wanted him because she needed to prove to herself that no tie was more sacred than experience. Maybe she wanted him because he'd done what she couldn't – he'd subjugated himself and opted for children, he'd taken a risk on a different kind of love. Something she found irresistible about him was that he spoke as though not qualified to assess the value of his own choices, as though he knew there could be no certainty from the inside. Even though he described his children with a softness that seemed to buff away the hardest edges of his life, it was clear that paternal love had not made him immune to the harmful forces of the world, nor had it been enough to keep him and Yvonne together. He was the proof Amy needed that no one thing could save you, and yet, hadn't he still found tranquillity, at long last? She was jealous of him that night, because she wanted that kind of tranquillity for herself, and it turned out that he was willing to spend three nights with her, assuring her that it would come.

Buoy wants to retrieve the sock from the totipotent mass. Amy lets her forage for a while, then catches herself on – imagine the uproar when Buoy shits a rancid sock on the kitchen floor. She leads the dog out of the wreck and onto the beach, away from the tetric stench of the tin sarcophagus. Back in the limitless temple of air and sea, Buoy seems less crazed, and the two walk in happy harmony along the sand, the intensity of their shared adventure quickly diluted in Buoy's nose by fresh odours.

She's always tried to foster a sanguine attitude about death, in the hope that her emotions might take their cue from her performed rationality. Death happens, after all. Happens constantly, in fact. It's happening all over the world, and people hate it, though not for the right reasons. Children are killed by drone strikes and military occupations and austerity-wrought starvation, but that's not the issue most people take – people don't mind that countless, faceless others are dying in genocides across the world. What they mind is that death will one day come for them. What they mind is that one day *they* will have to die.

It seems strange to her, in many ways, that he didn't leave a note – for the kids' sake, for Sasha's. For Yvonne's, even. But maybe it makes sense. Maybe he'd simply had enough of trying to make words bear the weight.

She hopes it was peaceful for him, at the end. She hopes that Father Spinola was right, and that there is a serenity to be found, beyond this life. She hopes that his mind was still, and that there wasn't too much fear. She doesn't feel much by way of fear, yet, at the mass they've found in her right breast – in some ways, it's nothing to do with her, it's just another alien process in a body.

The biopsy didn't yield the results they wanted, the doctor said. He was very careful, very kindly, very cagey. She imagined how Yvonne might have phrased it, had it been her cousin delivering the news: 'Stage three, Amy. It's stage three. Do you know what that means, Amy? Stage three? Listen, Amy. This is precisely what it means, Amy.' Never any room for misinterpretation, that was Yvonne's way. She probably thinks ambiguity is a carcinogen. Even with this gentler approach, though, it wasn't so hard to decipher the words behind the words. Tumour – from the Latin *tumere*, 'to swell'. Nothing swell about it, really. She laughs out loud. A single, hard laugh, into the wind. God, it must be wretched, doing what Yvonne does, trying to administer clarity amidst the impenetrable fog of desperation and denial. She tries to calm her mind. No point thinking about it now – one death at a time, one funeral at a time. She looks out to the indifferent sea – *not weighing hope against the weight of the water.* She lets Buoy off the leash for the last stretch of the walk, and the ageing dog regains her youth, bouncing and careening over the sand.

She doesn't mind going back to the beach with Yvonne after lunch – these aren't days for efficiency. It's better if Yvonne doesn't see the shipwreck at the beginning of their walk, though – she'll only start fretting, and that fretting will eclipse any benefit the walk might otherwise have. Amy insists on the long way round, and as they stroll down the beach, Amy steals glances at her cousin, who wears her paradoxes so openly she might as well be three people. She's currently fretting about the chicken, and Amy lets her tire herself out on the subject, offering nothing. She wonders how Yvonne feels about the arc of her life. It seems to be the fundamental principle of motherhood that you're not allowed to regret anything, however tangential, if it contributed in any small way to the existence of your children. Amy gets why this is vital, but she can't imagine how it must feel to be denied the option of a frank appraisal of your own existence. Amy's made a lot of mistakes, but at least she has the privilege of calling them mistakes, without guilt — she didn't tell Geoffrey to fuck off when he told her that her work wasn't interesting; she didn't visit her ageing parents enough before they died; she didn't let anyone talk her out of this fucking fringe. She got drunk the night before her interview for the editor job. She spent too many months in Beth and Theresa's spare room, gazing at the horrible Neruda and wasting time on self-pity. She was cruel — appallingly cruel — to Jess, the love of her life, when Jess's only crime was changing her mind. She allowed sadness to make her selfish. She slept with her cousin's ex-husband then barely spoke to him in the years after. She wishes she'd handled each of these instances differently, but she's allowed to wish that, because none of her decisions brought about a new person, apart from the newest version of herself.

This is why she admires Yvonne so much, because motherhood isn't just a sacrifice in all the obvious ways, you also give up so much of your right to regret. The only things you can regret are the ways you've hurt your children, and Amy can't imagine there's much catharsis in that. How do you assess a life where you didn't get much of what you wanted, where you frequently made missteps and gaffes, but you *did* get children? Anna is brilliant, obviously – a touch precocious and self-righteous, but mostly brilliant – and Gemma is becoming more enigmatic by the day; as for Matthew, Amy has always found it difficult to take teenage boys seriously, but he might well become interesting at some point. Is any of it enough, though? What of the disappointments? How do motherhood and personal disappointment coexist?

They leave their imprints on the damp sand. Yvonne seems on the cusp of saying something meaningful, and Amy is so keen to encourage it that she forgets herself in the process and almost reveals something, almost fucks everything up. She freezes for a second, wrapping her thumbs in the folds of her enveloping dress. She feigns insouciance and resumes walking, and a few moments later the wreck appears in front of them, and Yvonne, reliably, overreacts. The threat of a real conversation vanishes in the wreck's depths, and Amy tries not to see her own future in its darkness. After a while the agonising becomes a bit redundant, and Amy tries to neutralise Yvonne's intensity with indifference, which only aggravates Yvonne further. Instead, Amy puts her arm around Yvonne's shoulder and forcibly turns her away from the stimulus. She points out a luminescent flake of light on the sea's horizon, run through with the afternoon sun's jewellery. In and among the flecks of gold coating the water are bronze and blue and white. The swatch dances for them, wiggling on the waves. There are secrets worth keeping, Amy reminds herself, if it allows two people to share a moment with the sea. She takes a deep inhale, trying not to feel it as a disturbance in her breast. The world owes them nothing, but still this.

A tapas restaurant in Bath, 2004. Small discs loaded with charred Padrón peppers and pucks of red chorizo. Her and Jess's favourite spot for a semester.

'Jess?'

'What's up, love?'

'I have a question, which is not a trap. It's not meant to catch you out in any way.'

'Okay.'

'I just want to know what you think.'

'Okay.'

'So, you don't believe in free will, right?'

'I'm not sure I've ever put it in such stark terms as that, but I think there's sufficient evidence to suggest that all our actions are predetermined by social and biological processes.'

'If that's the case, why do we bother going to marches and rallies and protests? If everything is predetermined, then what's the motivation to be politically engaged, to try and be an ethical and thoughtful inhabitant of the earth?'

'Well, see, this is where the free-will conversation kind of eats itself, because if there is no free will, then we've not decided to do anything. We're not making the decision to try and be decent people.'

'Oh yeah. Shit.'

'I guess, though –'

'What?'

'I guess that even though there's so much evidence to the contrary, I have to believe that there's enough mystery arising from the question of consciousness to suggest there *might* be free will. If free will is a thing, then it's happening in there, in that space where nothing is understood.'

'Plus, I suppose it's harder for us to have a conversation about *anything* if it all gets shut down by the likelihood of choicelessness.'

'That too.'

'Do you think you choose to love me?'

'What do you mean?'

'Like, if we presuppose that free will exists, do you think love is a choice you make, or do you think it's unavoidable. Do you think you could choose to not love me?'

'I don't think I could choose, at will, to not love you, but I think I choose *how* to love you.'

'The choices you've been making so far are great ones.'

'Well, likewise.'

'Nyaw.'

'And what about you? Do you think you choose to love me?'

'I think I do, you know. I think I chose to allow myself to fall in love with you, just as you did me, just as I think either of us could choose at any moment to leave the other.'

'Why would either of us choose that, though?'

'I think if there was an extended period where we weren't being good to one another, then one of us would make the choice, in spite of love, for us to be apart. And I suppose over time then we'd have to try and choose to no longer love each other, just to make it bearable.'

'Okay, well how about we simply don't stop being good to one another?'

'Fine by me. I just hope that free will is real and it's not beyond our control. I'd hate to be forced by social and biological processes to be horrible to you.'

'Yeah, that would suck.'

All weekend the house on Gollan Hill has felt perilous on its foundations, ill-equipped to bear the weight of its inhabitants' unspoken, innumerable burdens. At what point does silence cease to be the safer option? At what point does it become too late to learn the language of candour?

That's the thing about this place: it might seem simpler, and cannier, to ignore the symptoms, but the refusal of history is not the same as a lack thereof – the tree falls whether you listen or not.

One of her favourite things about art is how it alters the experience of sadness. When she was a teenager she would lie in her room for hours, sobbing and staring at something that wasn't there. Her sadness was a place she could visit, from which she'd return exhausted but with no time having passed at all. In her twenties, she found a new place to go – she found a new way to warp and distort grief's duration, she could eclipse hours of misery with the pale grain of a page. Nothing releases her from herself like writing; she's never a less clearly defined person than when she inhabits language, when she is allowed to forgo her body and tap into the compulsive vibrancy of poetry. As long as she has poetry, life's limits are not her emotions – she has a way through fear, through unhappiness. As long as she has this to return to.

She wakes early, the morning of the funeral. She can hear someone clattering about downstairs, so she goes to the window and watches Matthew descending the steps in running shoes and shorts. It's going to rain. She pulls her long dress from one of the squashy hold-alls and lifts it aloft. Wrinkles run vascular across the cotton. She sighs.

She drapes the dress over a hanger Yvonne left out for her and takes it into the bathroom. The rest of the family remains behind their closed doors, and though Amy is supposed to be third in the morning's rota, nobody else seems to be awake, so she decides to turn the immersion on and go first. This way the water will be hot by the time Yvonne walks her stiff hip to the shower.

She hangs the dress on the door of the stall, then turns the dial. She washes quickly, avoiding touching her breasts. Once clean, she wraps her hair in a towel and returns to the study. She sits down at the desk in her dressing gown, positions a small make-up mirror so that her face is in direct sunlight. She rubs serum and moisturiser into her skin, pulling her face taut. She removes the towel and combs out her tiny, stupid fringe, then wraps it in a pink roller. Her chemotherapy is scheduled to start next month, so they'll see what becomes of her stupid fringe then. She leaves the rest of her hair to curl naturally around her shoulders, then she retrieves her laptop from her bag and opens it to the Word doc with the new poems. She starts writing. Death is frightening, but stasis is worse.

Matthew

The woman is in his room again.

He knows she's not, objectively, but try telling that to his heart rate, to his brittle muscles, to the panic bothering his eyes. Beyond the safety of his blue and green striped duvet, in the dark corner between the wardrobe and the wall, the woman in the black dress and shoes is standing upright, pointed towards his bed, towards his shaking form. The more thought he gives to her, the more likely it is that she will start walking towards him, and he knows that if he peeks out from under the bedsheets he will see her stumble on the rug and crouch, just for a second, like a dog about to attack, before regaining her balance and resuming her laborious, endless approach. He knows all this because it's happened the last two nights, and there seems to be no guarantee it won't happen every night for the rest of his life, because he can't stop: he can't stop conjuring her into his room, he can't stop summoning her into the dark.

It was David's idea to watch *Kairo*. His dad has a whole drawer full of old DVDs, and when David said they wanted a horror film, his dad rifled through and produced this one, declaring it one of the greatest horror films ever made. Matthew was sceptical at first, because it had subtitles, but when he suggested they watch the American remake instead Rachel said that she'd seen it already and it was shit. Ciara and Jason wanted to stream *Snowpiercer*, but Miss Gault had made the class watch *The Day After Tomorrow* across three Geography lessons, 'as a treat', and now Matthew can't stop reading articles about permafrost thaw, so he sided with David and Rachel and *Kairo* won out.

Something that hadn't occurred to him about a subtitled film is that it's harder to look away from. For most of it, it was fine – he could focus on reading, rather than looking too intently at what was happening above the words – but then the scene with the woman happened, and there was no dialogue. There was just her.

MATTHEW

In the scene, Toshio Yabe goes to Taguchi's apartment and finds a door, sealed over with red tape. He breaks the tape and goes inside, and across a long room cast in geometric panels of shadow he notices the shape of a woman. Her head and shoulders are obscured by darkness – you can only tell it's a person at all from the pale, slender shins, ending in a pair of black pumps, and the pale hands protruding from black dress sleeves. Matthew missed her too, at first, on the dark screen, in David's dark loft. Then Ciara said, 'Oh fuck, look,' and he saw her.

The woman doesn't do anything at first, so you might even think the film has frozen, if not for the music. Then the camera cuts away, to Yabe's terrified expression, which is something that has always worked to compound Matthew's fear, any time he watches a horror film – the confirmation that what's happening is terrifying is half of what terrifies him, and when he saw Yabe's wide, appalled eyes he gripped a pillow to his chin and wished with all his might for the scene to be over, for the film to give them a reprieve. Then the camera returned to the woman, and she started walking. Towards Yabe, towards Matthew.

Her gait was slow and strange – not like she'd been filmed in slow-motion, but like the normal laws of gravity and kinetic energy didn't apply. Her feet seemed to step upon the air, as though finding resistance, and they landed lightly, like no impact was involved at all. Her arms took looping swings out from her body, and it was almost magisterial for a second, if unsettling – like she was an astronaut, traversing the concourse to board a rocket. This, Matthew thought, wasn't so bad. This he could cope with, this was just about okay.

Then she took another step, and he wasn't sure if she had lost her footing or if she was lowering her body into a crouch deliberately. Her right knee bent deeply and her whole body dropped low to the floor. Her arms flew out at deliberate angles, and it looked like she was preparing to go on all fours, to break into a gallop that would transport her across the room within seconds. Matthew couldn't help it – he let out a pathetic little yip, and Ciara laughed uncertainly. But then, the woman steadied herself, at that low angle; her arms and legs straightened, and she returned to standing, but the worst thing was that throughout this horrible interlude her face didn't move. She didn't dip her head to see what her body was doing – she never looked at the floor so she could right herself, she never looked away from Yabe, from Matthew. Her face remained half-hidden, but the half that was visible was poorly lit in dim beige, so her features were indistinct.

MATTHEW

Her eye was a deep black concave in her skull. Upright again, her face became once more cloaked in shadow, and she resumed her walk. The problem was that the walk was now so much worse, because Matthew had seen her long limbs, arching from her body in angular tendrils, he'd seen her expressionless face and her deep black cavity of an eye, never not focussed on him as she'd briefly dropped to that predator's position, and even though the rest of the film was manageable, comparatively, and even though they'd each had a go on David's drums afterwards, the woman never left Matthew's mind. Even when he got home, he couldn't stop himself from fixating on the half-moon of her vacant, inhuman visage. It's that face that now lives in the corner of his room, just waiting to be summoned by the strength of his thinking.

Sunday night is once more marked by interruption. Curled in a ball, he sleeps in nervous bursts, waking again and again to new layers of sweat on his skin, congealing over old layers. He just wants it to be day, and when he looks at his phone and sees that it is 6 a.m. he feels a relief that surpasses his exhaustion, because he's made it. He darts across the room to throw open the heavy curtains, and the sun, trapped in a bonnet of grey cloud, purifies his bedroom, filling every inch with pewter light. He pulls on his shorts and opens Spotify on his phone, syncing it with his huge headphones. Kitted up, he flings himself downstairs. Buoy is sniffing around Anna's bedroom door, so he gives her back a scratch then escorts her to the kitchen. He refills her water dish and sneaks her a treat from the cupboard, and while she's gnawing on it in an ungainly way, he slips down the hall and out the front door. He does static lunges on the porch then jogs down the steps, feeling the mesh of his shorts stick and unstick to the clammy flesh of his thighs and balls. He is halfway down the steps before the day's itinerary assembles itself in the forefront of his mind: Dad's funeral. A moan squeezes itself from somewhere beneath his diaphragm. He sets his jaw and continues towards the beach, trying to focus on the task at hand.

Mum told him last night to steer clear of the shipwreck, and at this directive he kept his face neutral, as though he was just learning of the wreck's existence, because for some unfathomable reason his sisters thought it should be kept secret. Yesterday morning, when they sat swaddled in blankets in the front room, Anna paused the TV to tell him about the ship, and then she paused the TV again, two minutes later, to tell him not to say anything. 'Seriously, Matthew, keep it to yourself.' Gemma was nodding along with a stupid, serious expression on her face, as though she and Anna had concluded together that it was some matter of monumental importance, but then when *she* kept trying to pause the TV to talk to Anna about something else, Anna kept brushing her off – 'It's not really my problem, Gem. Just chill out, it'll be fine.' He tried to ask Gemma what was going on, but they both just told him to shut up. He felt pretty pissed off then, so he went upstairs to play the Switch. He thought about telling Mum about the wreck, to get back at them: why should he keep their random secrets when they won't even tell him what's going on? Further, what was even the point of keeping the shipwreck a secret, when Mum saw it that afternoon anyway? It was clearly just another item on Anna's weird agenda, and Gemma went along with it because she's obsessed with Anna, which strikes Matthew as deeply embarrassing.

Matthew gets that Anna's cool – she left home when she was only a bit older than he is, and now she lives in London and writes for magazines and stuff – he gets it, but it's still all a bit much, isn't it? This carrying on like their mum is some colossal cunt gets old. She's mad, obviously, but then all his friends' mums are mad (apart from Ciara's, who let them paint Ciara's bedroom that time, and didn't even seem to care that they made a total mess of it). Sure, Mum is angsty, but then maybe she should be. Isn't there plenty to be angsty about? He doesn't understand these random acts of exclusion, of complicity at their mum's expense. Like, what's the point? That being said, he didn't tell Mum about the wreck — anything for an easy life. That's why he didn't go for a run yesterday — so he wouldn't have to see the wreck and then pretend not to have. He just wants some accord in the house, which has been tense all weekend with its incompatible personalities. Ever since Mum told him that Dad was dead it's felt like the house is on the cusp of fracturing, like all its life and matter might disperse into the ether. That's why he kept the secret of the washed-up bit of boat, to try and foster peace. He kept it in the same way he's keeping the secrets of Gemma, who he heard puking her guts up in the early hours of Saturday, and who spent all of dinner last night poking her food and trying to catch Anna's eye. And then there's Anna, who he saw scampering into the bathroom on Saturday night, tearful and covered in nasty, poisonous-looking black stuff, like those images of dying sea-birds. He's keeping his mum's secrets, who he overheard hyperventilating

MATTHEW

in the kitchen while Anna was in the shower, just when he was entertaining going downstairs to hang out with her and Amy — she was screeching about how horribly everyone treats her, which gave him a hollow, cold feeling in his sternum. She's not wrong, to be honest — Anna treats her like shit, half the time — but why does she have to be so dramatic about everything? As for Amy, he heard her crying behind the study door this morning, which was especially strange, because Amy never cries — she just makes jokes he doesn't understand and looks at them like they're insects she's gathered in a jar. Also, it's not like she even knew his dad that well, so why is *she* so upset?

There are so many things he doesn't understand, not least why his dad is dead. Why is his dad dead? He hasn't asked, because it feels like you can't ask anything in this house without someone flying off the handle. It's all too fraught and too stressful, so he says nothing. This is what he knows how to do, in this house full of women. He knows to say nothing.

So, there's the wreck. He gives it a cursory glance. It's basically an oversized tin, ripped open at one end and filthy and gross-looking. Why do any of them care so much? Did his mum really think he was going to climb on top of it and immediately injure himself? He's not a child.

He goes for a quick loop, taking in its metal girth and cruddy angles. He adjusts his headphones, burly like two crumpets, over his ears. He performs a few more lunges, inching across the beach. He pauses at the wreck's opening, contemplating the vantablack wormhole of its insides. He stares for too long, and the woman answers his invitation – the pale details of her hands and shins start to glow dimly in the ship's depths. He swallows, takes a step back. She starts her slow approach. He shakes his head and turns away. 'Fuck no, fuck this.' He sets off across the sand, too fast at first, too eager to get away from her, from the home she's made inside his head.

He's grateful, in some ways, for the ghost woman. Too scared to illuminate his phone screen in case she manifests in its corona, he's been forced to take a couple of nights away from the articles on BBC Future and ETH Zürich and *New Scientist*, the ones that expose in ruthless detail what's happening to the world. Before he got put in Miss Gault's class for Geography, he watched TikToks before bed, and it was all American siblings having secret incest sex or bald men explaining how most actresses are secretly trans. It wasn't funny or interesting, but at least he could fall asleep without panicking. It makes him feel insane, sometimes, that nobody around him seems to be panicking. What use is any of the day-to-day bullshit if in a few years they'll all die in a flood? Their house is practically *on* the sea, and yet none of them seem bothered by the sea levels or the changes to the water cycle or the mass species death happening *right* now, just below the ocean's surface, because of rising temperatures and algal blooms and suffocating sediment deposits. Meanwhile, his mum is worried the shipwreck might be unsafe – what about where the wreck came from? What, does she think it's a coincidence that a big chunk of boat just happened to wash up now? Is she stupid? Is everyone stupid?

He doesn't want to have to worry about any of this – he wants to pass his GCSEs and then his A Levels. He wants to go somewhere far away from here, somewhere inland. He wants to get a degree and a girlfriend and a flat and a job. He wants to live a normal life, and not have to worry about his family or the sinking earth. At least the ghost woman isn't fucking real, at least he can keep reminding himself of that. He nods, newly convinced of her harmlessness. He speeds up.

* * *

But then, imagining shit that's not real, allowing it to take up your whole life and terrorise you… Where does that get you? Mum was so unlike herself, when she told him about Dad. Normally, he would have trusted her to tell him the truth, because she never shuts up about 'perspective', 'getting perspective', 'having some perspective'. She used to come home from the hospital with all these grim stories about death and disease, usually as a way to stop Gemma complaining about her hair. It was a bit much, to be honest, and made him feel like there was nothing that could ever be wrong enough in his life to warrant sympathy, because someone elsewhere was always dying. At least it felt like the truth though. All she's said about Dad is that he struggled for a long time 'with sadness'. Like, what does that even mean? And is that what *this* is, this heaviness in his chest and this carousel of unbidden images in his mind? This feeling like in every direction there's a different, impossible enemy he can't ignore? He goes even faster, his sock-like runners thumping the sand, his quads undulating. How do you tell the difference between feeling sadness and struggling with it? What's normal? And can you even tell from inside it?

* * *

MATTHEW

His pace catches up with him. It's not sustainable. He slows to a jog, then a walk, then he stops. He folds at the knees and gulps the damp air. It starts to rain, and he's grateful, though for all he knows it might never stop. He unfurls his vertebrae and takes his phone out of his pocket. There are messages in the group chat, wishing him good luck today. He ignores them and picks a new song, the one that always helps him find the right rhythm. He resumes running, and this time his tempo is perfect, simpatico with the music. He concentrates on that, pictures himself a machine, functional and system-driven. Every movement is dictated by a network of interlocking bearings, axles, springs, rivets. The engine runs as it should, and he moves, crafted for this singular purpose. The beach unrolls before him like a treadmill, and the rain acts as a coolant. He tips his head to the sky and welcomes a face full of wet, and the horrible shipwreck, his weird family, the funeral, the breaking world – all are banished to a derelict district of his mind. Reverse osmosis happens, and the sweat leaves his pores to intermingle with the water on his skin. It'll all be okay. He'll turn eighteen eventually, and then he'll do it – he'll leave. He'll see his family less frequently and they'll all be happier for it, because it's easier to keep secrets when you're apart. He'll return from runs like this, to a home he shares with friends, or with a girlfriend, or with nobody. It'll be great, even if it's with nobody. He thinks back to the ghost woman, pursuing him slowly from the black nidus of the beached boat. If she wants it, she can come get it – she can try him, and just see what fucking happens. Yeah – what's she gonna do? Stupid bitch. Stupid fucking bitch.

He smiles into the downpour, and the music drives his legs forward, away from everything. He loves this – running, by himself. He's always been happy by himself. He's always loved the rain.

Miss Gault is new to the school; she just started this year. She's young, relative to Matthew's other teachers, and pretty. She wears a pale green, shin-length, silky skirt sometimes, and it seems to react with the pale flecks in her pale eyes. It was about a month ago that the pertinent details about her began to percolate through the school: Miss Gault is a former Rose of Tralee, and not only that, she used to model. It didn't take long for David's older brother and his friends to apply their invigorated curiosity to the details of Miss Gault's past, and within a day they'd retrieved a picture from the website of a Dublin-based boutique: Miss Gault, several years younger but mostly unchanged,

MATTHEW

posing in a tiny white bikini and a floppy sun hat. They printed out the picture and circulated it around the school. David got his hands on a copy, which he brought to the canteen before first bell, scrunched up in his blazer pocket. They'd huddled over it, though the quality was quite poor – a printout of a screenshot of the original picture.

Ciara said she couldn't figure out why Miss Gault was bothering with teaching, when she had a body like that. She said that if it were her, she'd be in Dubai or something, married to someone rich and spending most of her time on a yacht. Rachel countered this by saying it's not like Miss Gault looks like that now – she's older and fatter, and back then she wasn't even *that* good-looking, she just looked anorexic. Jason said that Rachel was obviously just jealous, because Miss Gault was still a hundred times better-looking than her. This isn't true, but Matthew nevertheless thought it was right of Jason to say it, because Rachel was being horrible. Matthew didn't say anything, and this prompted David to nudge the picture towards him and say he could take it home to wank over if he wanted. Matthew told him to fuck off, and everyone laughed, and then Mr Hamilton came in to rally everyone towards class, so Matthew grabbed the picture and stuffed it into his bag. It's on his desk at home now, folded between the pages of his Statistics textbook. It's been there for about three weeks. He never really looks at it, but he's not sure what to do with it, because the recycling bin only gets emptied once a week, so his mum or Gemma would definitely find it, curled among the ready-meal sleeves and the old catalogues, but he feels strange about putting it in the normal bin, partly because it feels disrespectful to turn Miss Gault into rubbish, but also because Miss Gault gave Jason a hard time for not recycling the packet his sandwiches had come in.

He never wanked over it, despite what David thinks. The picture just doesn't excite him, in that way — for starters, Miss Gault's face is now permanently associated in his mind with all the horrors of their dying planet, but also, for the most part, she's been so nice to him.

He knows that women have quite a bad time, generally speaking — Gemma seems to always be bloated or in discomfort, or on the cusp of being bloated or in discomfort. Sometimes she has to lie on the floor with a hot water bottle hugged to her pelvis, and once, when he got up to use the toilet in the middle of the night, it was clear that Gemma had already been there, because the bowl was full of blood. Not just liquid blood, either, but a round lozenge of a

MATTHEW

clot, with tendrils like a sea creature. It was disgusting, and he thought about waking her up to tell her to flush away her mess, but he didn't, because he's never, to his knowledge, lost that amount of blood in one go, never mind doing it once a month. Rachel has endometriosis, which she has dedicated her Instagram to talking about, and though David initially suggested that he and Matthew and Jason watch some of her reels to make fun of her, Matthew thinks they all just ended up feeling a bit guilty, not to mention horrified.

And all of this before you even get onto rape. It's like *every* woman is going to get raped. Maybe that's an exaggeration – it's hard to know. Sometimes, Matthew sees Instagram reels where girl runners talk about how they can't go out jogging at night, and most of the top comments are from men, saying that they wouldn't touch the girls if they were paid to, that the girls are kidding themselves if they think any man would even want to rape them. Even if this were true, it's not a logic that would apply to Miss Gault, Matthew thinks, because she's objectively beautiful. This is another reason why the printed-out pictures of her made him feel uncomfortable, because if it's true that most women are going to get raped, then it's probably horrible to be reminded that your place of work is filled with people who think you're hot, and who might decide to rape you at some point.

The pictures were put up in secret places across the school – there was one on the music noticeboard, one in the window of the prefect room, a couple in the sports hall vestibule. It must have been some undertaking, putting them up without being caught, but they didn't last long. The pictures were taken down after a day or two, and Matthew expected some kind of school-wide reckoning, but it never came. Miss Gault kept showing up to class, seemingly unfazed, and Matthew was confused, because on the one hand he felt sorry for her, because she'd been violated, but on the other hand he hated her a bit, because it seemed like every day she was telling them things that he couldn't leave behind in class, facts and statistics that have followed him home and dominated his thoughts. He thought at the very least the photo saga might require her to take a few days off, to pause her relentless monologue of doom. Seriously, what the fuck does she expect *him* to do about it? He can't halt the rising tides, he can't re-salt the sea or outlaw carbon emissions. He got Mum to drive him into town one day so he could go to a sit-in in the Guildhall Square, but when he got there it was just a herd of badly dressed teenagers, brandishing amateur signs that said things like, 'There is no Planet B,' as though *that* was going to achieve anything. He was too embarrassed to sit down with them, so he skived off. He took a bus to Jason's, and the two of them spent the afternoon taking penalties at one another.

Football is pretty good, to be fair, at taking his mind off things. His dad wasn't a normal football fan, but he was interested in it in unusual ways – he was able to relay to Matthew in excruciating detail the events of the 2003 FA Cup Final between Arsenal and Southampton. He had a real thing about that game, was always referencing 'young Chris Baird from Rasharkin', a Southampton midfielder, even though Southampton didn't win the match. Matthew was a baby at the time, so couldn't exactly contribute any impressions of his own, but it was nice to hear about it, nevertheless. It was hard to infer whether his dad had been happy or disappointed about the result, or any result – he was more interested in the schematics of matches: who had played, who was injured, how the score had affected either club's standing more broadly. Matthew used to go to an Under-13 skills club every Tuesday, before he realised he didn't like team sports, and sometimes his dad would drive him home, asking if he was going to be the next 'young Chris Baird from Rasharkin'. It always made Matthew laugh, and if he'd been worried that quitting football would disappoint his dad he needn't have been – before long he was being asked if he was the new 'young Mark Carroll from Knocknaheeny'.

It felt easy, having an interest in football – it was something he and Dad could watch without having to discuss anything else. Matthew hates it when people ask him about himself. His life is so boring, and it makes him *feel* boring to have to talk about it, but you can't exactly get into the fact that sea turtles are facing extinction because of temperature-dependent sex determination when one of your mum's awful friends asks you how school is going. Who the fuck *cares* how school is going?

Something else happened, a few months ago, that he's been feeling strange about, especially in light of the Miss Gault bikini pictures. His school has this antiquated, stupid tradition, involving fancy ties – if you're a member of a team, or a club, or band, or if you're exceptionally good at exams, you get to wear a different tie from everyone else. The tie has silver stripes, instead of the standard blue ones. It's the kind of thing he would never normally care about, except that they give out the ties at a special assembly that happens during fifth and sixth period,

MATTHEW

so everyone receiving one gets to skip class and has a longer than usual lunch break. It's normally just lower and upper sixth students who go, because they've been around long enough to 'prove their commitment' to the school, as Mr McCann puts it at every opportunity. Mr McCann is an alcoholic, and maybe even a nonce – he definitely has a noncey look to him, his face is mostly slimy widow's peak and huge yellow teeth.

A list of all those receiving the silver ties is pinned to the announcements board a week before the ceremony, so that those people know not to go to class. This year, Matthew and Jason's names were on the list, for services to athletics. He thought it was strange, because he's only been doing cross country for a year and half, and even though he's good, it didn't change the fact that he and Jason were the only fifth years on the list. He told Jason he reckoned it was a mistake, but Jason said it didn't matter if it was a mistake – they'd get to miss Geography, plus they'd be first in line for the toastie counter at lunchtime. Matthew remained unconvinced, because he didn't like the idea of Mr McCann giving them grief, so he went to the office and asked one of the maternal secretaries for her advice. She said she'd make enquiries, but that she hoped it wasn't a mistake, because in her opinion

Matthew deserved one of the fancy ties, which was nice of her to say.

He called back in at lunchtime, and she said she'd checked, and unfortunately it was a mistake; the silver ties are only for sixth formers. He relayed this to Jason and Jason gave him a shove and called him a pain in the hole, but otherwise it was fine – just a normal afternoon.

The following week arrived, and then it was the day of the tie ceremony. Matthew and Jason were on their way to fifth period when they were intercepted by a friend of David's brother, who asked them what the fuck they were playing at, didn't they know they were supposed to be at the assembly? Matthew tried to explain that it was a mistake, but David's brother's friend said he didn't give a fuck – he'd been sent to fetch them, so they'd better get a fucking move on. They followed him to the hall, both a bit giddy at this reversal of fortunes. When they got there, McCann was in a drill stance on the stage, directing throngs of people to their seats. The orchestra and jazz band members occupied the first two rows, then there were the athletes, then the 'academically gifted'. David's brother's friend strode to the front of the hall and announced that he'd fetched Matthew and Jason, then

MATTHEW

went to his seat, abandoning them to the empty aisle between the rows of chairs. Matthew felt less excitable and more embarrassed, now, because their late arrival had attracted the curiosity of everyone in the hall. McCann paused his militant shepherding to look at them. He consulted his clipboard, then looked at them again. He asked them what year they were in, and Matthew felt something inside him plummet, as though the wires and tubes responsible for holding his stomach in its correct position had snapped. He said nothing, and Jason said, 'Fifth year, sir,' because nobody at school calls any teacher by their actual name – it's all 'sir' and 'miss'. McCann consulted his clipboard again, chewing on his lips with his oversized sheep's teeth. After a pause he said, 'You shouldn't be here,' and because the room had lapsed into silence, everyone heard this, and a couple of people giggled. Matthew hauled his voice up from where it had retreated inside him and said, 'But we were just told to come,' and then McCann gave him a look of greasy derision, one that made Matthew think that if McCann *is* a nonce, then he must just be one of the internet ones, because how could anyone let a man with this awful a face get close to a child? Matthew looked down at his feet, and then McCann spoke again.

'If either of you had any sense,' he said, 'you would have realised that your name was on the list in error. You clearly just wanted to skive off class. Get back to wherever it is you're supposed to be, and stop wasting my time.' Matthew wanted to point out that what McCann had said was stupid, because *either* he and Jason had no sense, and hadn't realised the list was a mistake, *or* they wanted to skive off class – it couldn't be both. He said nothing, and he and Jason walked down the aisle, and as they did Matthew could hear a few of the older athletes laughing, and as they reached the double doors Matthew felt such a profound sense of rage that he wanted to turn around. He wanted to scream, he wanted to scream and then punch and kick the faces of every cunt in that room, because how dare they treat him this way? He and Jason walked through the empty corridors to Geography, Jason laughing at what a prick McCann was, but Matthew feeling too angry to laugh. Matthew simmering and clenching and unclenching his fists.

When they got to Geography, Miss Gault was in the middle of drawing a diagram of radiative exchange. She asked them why they were late, but when Jason tried to explain he didn't do it properly – he didn't capture the injustice of the sorry, sordid incident – so it just sounded like they'd been chancing their arm, like they were just two eejits who wanted to skip class. Miss Gault looked at them with raised eyebrows and said that they had no business showing up so late, that it was disrespectful and lazy and that she wasn't impressed. She told them to go to their seats, and it was with such irritation in her voice that Matthew once again found himself wanting to scream at how unfair everything was. How *dare* she not realise that he and Jason weren't the ones at fault; how *dare* she speak to them like they were a couple of worthless fuckwits. What an absolute bitch.

He spent class stewing in a taut fury, and when lunch finally came around he recruited David, who never needs an excuse, into getting some revenge. They went to the boys' toilets and Matthew wrote, 'Miss Gault sucks Mr McCann's syphilitic cock,' in huge blue letters on a sheet of paper, and with David keeping watch he pinned it to the noticeboard in the Geography corridor. They then headed to the canteen, David slapping Matthew on the back and calling him a legend.

Like the photos, the piece of paper didn't stay up for long, but Matthew can't stop thinking about it. He keeps wondering if this was exactly the kind of impulse that made David's brother and his friends look for pictures of Miss Gault in her underwear; if

Matthew is just like one of those men who tells girl runners on Instagram that they're not good enough to be raped; if he's evil, beyond reproach. He thought about what his dad would say, if he ever found out. He even considered confessing, but then Miss Gault, stoic as ever, continued to teach them about the specifics of climate change, and now Matthew feels so frightened of about forty different things that a piece of paper with a stupid lie scrawled on it seems trivial, comparatively – especially if whoever found it decided to recycle it.

He slows on the approach to the old harbour at the beach's end. He performs a sweeping U-turn, adding in as much distance as he can. He feels his lungs emanating warmth within his chest.

How is he supposed to do his GCSEs in six weeks? He's getting something called special dispensation, which is a pity tariff for children with dead parents. He and Ciara read the guidelines on Friday night, and it's only for people whose parents have died in the six-month period before and during the exams, which struck him as being monumentally messed up. Ciara was really funny about it. She kept pretending to be an invigilator, ruling out people's bereavements on the basis of random technicalities.

MATTHEW

'Oh, I am sorry, little Perkins, but I'm afraid your mother died in a boat on the Atlantic, so by the rules of maritime law she's not TECHNICALLY a deceased person, she's a manatee, and we don't make allowances for manatees. Goodness ME, Queef, I'd simply LOVE to offer you some support, but I'm afraid according to the coroner's report your uncle voided his bowels one minute BEFORE midnight on December twelfth, and that means his death is about as pertinent to YOUR exams as that of the great Archduke Franz Ferdinand! Oh well, better luck next time!'

Rachel is widely regarded as the hot one, but Matthew thinks Ciara is much funnier, and pretty in her own way. He wishes she'd got to meet his dad – David met him once when Matthew offered him a lift home from the cinema, and the next week he'd told Jason that Matthew's dad was 'really starey and quiet', which made Matthew feel sad in a hard-to-understand way, because it was technically true. Ciara would get on with him, though – she'd be able to talk to him about how intelligent octopuses are or something. She's always watching documentaries about wildlife, and his dad would be interested because that's what he's like, he's just interested in things. Was.

* * *

The wreck appears again, its internal galaxy just out of view. Having already seen the woman climbing out of it, he now can't stop picturing it, and he feels his heart rate elevating as the wreck gets closer. He touches a hand to his ear to turn up the volume on his headphones, blasting his thoughts to shrapnel with heavy bass. It's okay, he reminds himself. It's not real. He tells himself to keep running. Just keep running. He decides that when he gets in, he'll lure Buoy into his bedroom with treats, even though he's not supposed to. He'll lie down on his bed in his wet gear, even though he's not supposed to do that, either. He'll let Buoy curl up on his chest, and the weight of her will anchor his thoughts. He'll stroke her little fluffy ears and it'll be okay. He'll be okay.

For all Mum's attempts to govern the morning, he arrives home to a frenzy. Amy didn't respect her appointed position in the shower schedule, and now Gemma is stomping around the kitchen in a fury because she thinks she won't have enough time to dry and curl her hair. Dad is dead, for fuck's sake, he wants to say, who gives a fuck about your hair? He says nothing. She asks Matthew if he thinks they'll have to call into the supermarket for anything on the way home, which is a weird question, and also

MATTHEW

how the fuck would he know? He asks her why she cares, and she just starts stomping around again, so he ignores her, dropping to the floor to ruffle Buoy's exposed belly. He crab-walks to the cupboard to get the sachet of meat-flavoured sticks, then returns to standing and rustles the plastic. Buoy rushes to his side, and they make a break for it, encountering his mum at the bottom of the stairs.

'Good run?'

'Yeah, it was okay.'

'Well done. Where are you going with her?'

'Nowhere, I was just going –'

'Things have descended into chaos here. Why don't you give me your wet things and I'll stick them on to wash while you shower?'

'No, it's okay, I was just going to –'

'Going to what? Gemma, the hairdryer is free now if you want to use it. It's in my room.' Gemma scurries past, red-faced. She nearly falls over Buoy.

'For God's sake, be careful, Gemma!'

Matthew throws himself backwards to make room. Gemma careens around the banister. 'Sorry! Sorry Buoy!' She flings her lanky torso upwards. Matthew bends over and pats Buoy's head. His mum looks at the treats in his hand.

'How many of those have you given her?'

'None, yet.'

'Well, give her one now and give me the packet, then go get your shower.'

He takes a stick and hands his mum the sachet. She heads for the kitchen. Buoy gazes after her with shining, rock-pool eyes, her tail wafting uncertainly.

'Here, Boo, what's this?' He plonks himself on the bottom stair, spreading his knees. Buoy sits between them, and he feeds her the treat. Her lovely pink gums appear and disappear as she chews it into nothingness. He leans forward and cuddles her solid little body in his arms, rubbing his nose against her ears and neck. When she has concluded the business of snacking, she licks his fingers and his knees. Her fur is long and fawn-coloured, run through with a lisle of white and brown. He breathes her in. She smells like a field.

'Matt! What did I *just* say? Get in the bloody shower, for God's sake!'

Mum drives them to the crematorium, which looks like a driving range. Surrounding it is a lush and sprawling cemetery. There are people milling about who aren't there for his dad's funeral but for other people's — his dad's is not the only funeral today, it's one of many. Everyone gets a time slot, sandwiched

MATTHEW

between other time slots. He doesn't like it, this conveyor belt of loss.

When he first got out of the car, he was shocked by the numbers, all uncanny in their black suits against the bright sunshine. He felt proud so many people were here to see his dad off, but when he said this to Gemma she said, 'Are you actually thick, Matt?' She's been such a bitch all weekend.

Sasha was hovering by the entrance when they arrived, gripping the hand of someone she introduced as her baby sister, even though the woman was at least forty. The woman proceeded to ensnare each of them in an intense and wide-eyed gaze, her head held at an unnatural angle, like she was trying to shake water from her ear. Matthew read once that you should adopt this pose with cats, that displaying your carotid artery lets animals know that you trust them. She awarded her 'deepest condolences' to them all, in a voice that was like Sasha's, but more full on. Anna and Gemma submitted to embraces from the woman, and as he waited for his turn, Sasha reached out a hand, and he didn't know what else to do but take it, and then they were hugging. He didn't mind. It was nice, even. Sasha had always had a kind of procedural positivity to her, like she'd been assigned to them by some benevolent but faceless organisation. He realised, as his hands found purchase in the rough linen of her dress, that he only really knew bits of her biography, that he had no idea what she liked or disliked. Now her boyfriend was dead, and he wondered if she felt angry, if she felt like she'd been abandoned. He and Gemma and Anna weren't her family – they'd never taken the piss out of her for not understanding a meme; she'd never shouted at them for crossing the road without looking. They probably could have been closer, had things been different. But then, if things were different, maybe she wouldn't have been a presence in their lives at all. When he came away from the hug, he told her he was sorry, and when she thanked him, he wondered if she knew he was apologising for the distance he's not even sure he would choose to close, were they to do this all over again. She said that his father was very proud of him, and it struck him that the conversations at funerals were just a scattering of non-sequiturs, nobody capable of responding to what was meant, everyone desperate to communicate something they weren't sure of.

Sasha told their mum that she looked beautiful, and Matthew thought the intuitive thing for Mum to do would be to return the compliment, because if Mum

MATTHEW

looked beautiful, then Sasha definitely did, with her shiny hair and long eyelashes. Instead, Mum did a kind of derisive snort, shaking her head about like a horse. Then she asked, 'Where are we sitting?' and he wondered if she was finally offering Sasha a 'we' because she knew there might be no cause to ever do so again. Sasha looked too grateful then, like she might make some weird pantomime of their shared circumstance, but she just whispered, 'We have the first two rows on the right,' and Mum nodded, extending her fingers to briefly graze Sasha's forearm.

Sasha had hired a humanist celebrant rather than a minister, because neither she nor Dad were religious. Matthew wasn't aware you could be that *un*religious – even the most pointless assemblies at school feature the Lord's prayer. The celebrant was a woman with bright blue glasses and a beige suit. Despite his misunderstanding of who was here for which funeral, the room was nevertheless fuller than Matthew expected, mostly with people Matthew didn't know, who his mum explained were doctors or pharmacists or the spouses of doctors and pharmacists – 'People from your dad's work, Matt, or mine.' She apologised to a woman with a severe grey haircut for the humanist celebrant, saying that she'd had no hand in the funeral planning and that, because Sasha is American, 'She's into a lot of New Age, spiritual nonsense.' The woman with the severe haircut laughed, as though in agreement. Matthew watched Amy roll her eyes.

There were a few Americans there, people who'd flown over. A guy with a beard so dense it seemed to act as ballast for his Zeppelin of a head bounded up to Amy and embraced her with huge declarations of condolence. Matthew thought he must have made a mistake, that he must have confused Amy for Mum, but then the man told Amy that it was wonderful to see her again, that he'd so enjoyed meeting her all those years ago, that it had meant so much to Thomas to see a familiar face from home, that the two of them had clearly shared such an easy rapport. It was strange for Matthew to hear someone refer to Dad by his first name. Thomas – in Gollan Hill he had always been spoken of as 'Dad' or 'your father'. Even Sasha just seemed to call him 'darling'.

Amy was quite rude to the bearded man, Matthew thought, given that he was so friendly – she rushed over his sentences to cut him short, then she started asking a lot of stupid and pointless questions about his flight. Something previously sleepy in Mum's eyes seemed to wake up, then, and she looked at Amy without saying anything, the awake and lively thing stalking careful circles across her pupils. The man with the metaphysical beard turned his attention to Mum then, asking if she was a friend of Thomas's. She stared at him, and Matthew was worried she was going to make some kind of scene, but she just said in a clipped way that she was the ex-wife, that Amy was her cousin. As the man's beard rippled in confusion, Amy said, 'Excuse me, Tad, it was nice to see you again,' and then forcibly guided Matthew to a pew, next to Anna and Gemma. He'd glanced back to see if Mum was following them, but she remained in the aisle, the creature in her eyes at odds with the stillness of her body.

The service was nice, even though he felt, as it was happening, like he was forgetting it, or like he wasn't experiencing the passage of time in the usual way. He tried to concentrate on what the woman in the blue glasses was saying, and when he managed to it seemed like she was correct on a lot of fronts. She kept saying that life is short, but nevertheless capable of being filled with great meaning, and he found himself wanting that to be true. She mentioned Matthew and Anna and Gemma by name, and then she talked for a while about Mum – she said that Dad was incredibly grateful to his former wife, Yvonne, for blessing him with three beautiful children, and for being a better and stronger and more reliable parent than he was. Sasha must have written that, which Matthew thought was decent of her. He glanced over at Sasha a few times. She looked glamorous and sad and thoughtful, like one of the Scottish Widows. He wondered if he would see much of her, after this. Not that he saw that much of her before, but she was always friendly, and Matthew was able to buy his big headphones with the money she and Dad gave him for Christmas. Sasha's dress was sleeveless, and she was by far the tannest person in the room. She cried a lot, but not in an over-the-top way, although Mum flashed a look in her direction every time she made the slightest noise. Mum was strange throughout the whole ceremony, like a current was running up from the floor and into her body. Matthew couldn't stop himself from crying a bit, and even though it was an okay time to be doing it, in the grand scheme of things, Amy made it so much worse by putting her arm around him, which depleted all his reserves of control. Anna didn't cry, but when Matthew looked over at her he almost flinched, for her expression was somehow that of someone experiencing the losses of everyone the world over, and it was so much worse than if she had been crying – hers looked to him like a sadness that might never be let go of. He didn't

MATTHEW

know what to do about it, so he looked away, pressing his arms into his sides for stability. Gemma kept touching her hair, which was embarrassing, so he focussed on trying to resist the effect of Amy's arm, which seemed specifically designed to tempt him towards collapse. He didn't look at Mum, because he could feel her volatile energy reverberating through the pew. He knew that whatever she was feeling was probably too complicated, and he didn't want to have to try and understand it. He directed his eyes forward, and tried once more to hear the nice things the humanist celebrant was saying. He liked the way she made Dad sound, like he was clever and resilient and meaningful in the world. If this was all New Age, spiritual nonsense, then maybe he would become a New Age, spiritual nonsarian. The windows of the crematorium hall were open to let in the late spring air, and the strongest aromas were those of furniture polish and freshly cut grass.

The long drive home is mostly silent. Amy makes a stupid joke about the tiny sandwiches, and nobody tries to laugh. The atmosphere isn't sad, though there is sadness within it. He isn't sure what it is, but it feels both oppressive and fragile, like its intensity is keeping something worse at bay.

The gathering afterwards felt a bit hectic after the relative calm of the service. Amy kept loading their table down with plates of vol-au-vents and tray bakes, even after Anna told her they'd had enough. Mum seemed to be working too hard at speaking to absolutely everyone, like she was scared they might forget about her, or underestimate her claim to proceedings. Sasha perched in the corner, eating very little and looking, to be fair to her, like a woman whose partner had died. When a group of Americans asked to join them, Amy excused herself, unearthing a fat box of cigarettes from her bag – Matthew tried to chain her to the table with his eyes, not sure how they were expected to deal with these strangers without her, but if she knew what he meant she ignored it, and then they were surrounded by inquisitors.

'So, what are the plans for college?'

'Can I get any of you kids a Guinness?'

'Any interest in the sciences?'

This last one was addressed solely to him, and he thought about Ciara, about how much he would have liked to hear her telling Dad about how cheetahs went through a population bottleneck thousands of years ago and now they're all related. He decided to tell the American man with the flat cap this, in lieu of anything better. The man said, 'Is that right?' but like it wasn't really a question, so then Anna said something about how population bottlenecking might be a thing in Ulster soon enough, the rate at which people were dying. Matthew didn't really understand what she meant, but shortly after the Americans went to the bar and didn't return, and then it was just the three of them. He preferred that. Anna nudged a couple of fifteens onto his and Gemma's plates, and they ate them in silence. Amy returned, dishevelled and smelling of wind and peat, and the four of them listened to the soundtrack of funeral murmurs. It wasn't so bad, that bit, he thought. It felt like they might all be thinking the same thing.

He stares out the window, trying to consolidate as many memories as he can, so that it matters, so that today matters. The afternoon sun has persevered, and as they finally reach Railway Road and follow the curve along the coast, he watches it land on the hills of Gweedore and sit atop them like an ornament. Soon, it will start to melt onto the dark flat, like the Flora does in the pan, only deeper and hotter in hue, more violent. He suddenly feels a pronounced resistance to going home. He doesn't want to go home. He can't say this, though, because it will incite an unbearable flurry of attention. He will be probed by four sets of inscrutable eyes, each with a different agenda. He can't bear it, but after several minutes of steeling himself, he asks if they can go for a walk on the beach. It's the first thing any of them has said for nearly an hour, and his voice feels like an intruder. He tries to say it nonchalantly, but he chokes – an unaccounted-for mass in his throat is threatening to break his voice in two. He fights it, spitting the words out, turning towards the window so that neither Gemma nor Anna can see that his eyes are watering, and when Mum, predictably – why always so predictable – says in a clipped voice that they need to go home so she can get started on the tea, something gives. His nose starts running, his eyes start watering. He doesn't understand what's happening in his face and body, but he rolls his eyes to the furry ceiling of the car to try and stop the tears. He pinches his right thigh through the thin fabric of his trousers and tells himself to catch himself on, because what the fuck is wrong with him? Why is he crying over not being allowed to go for a walk on the beach? And so, he's sitting there, trying to sniff quietly and infrequently, and he brings his hand across his face in a

MATTHEW

surreptitious motion he hopes will delay the most immediate leakages, while he tries to get himself under control. Gemma is doing something peculiar next to him – he can feel her shoulders, pressed against his own in the tightly packed back seat, tense up, and though he can't turn to look at her he can see out of the bottom corner of his soggy eyes that she's wringing her fingers, tensing and flexing them in a panic. He hears Anna mutter, 'Chill the fuck out, Gem,' and Gemma issues a hiss in response. Mum says, 'What's going on back there?' and Gemma says, in a voice not even he is convinced by, 'Nothing!' but rather than press the issue Mum just sighs, like everything in the world is a bother. The car takes the turn to begin ascending the winding, uneven road up to the house, and though he has managed to pause his despair, the water refuses to drain from the reservoirs behind his face – it pools, waiting for him to falter in his concentration. He pretends his sisters don't exist, focusses on keeping it together. The car ascends towards home. He just wanted to go to the beach.

From the moment they disembark the car, it seems to Matthew like a lot of things happen very quickly. A lot of things that, taken in isolation, might have remained usual, and innocuous, but on this day, for some reason, conspire to create something bigger than the sum of their parts.

First, his mum is slamming the car door. Amy calls to her but she ignores it, and then she's opening the front door and striding towards the kitchen in her purposeful way. Matthew and Gemma and Anna follow, and then Buoy is with them in the hall, unleashed from the world that shrinks when the family is not home, the world behind the shut kitchen door. Matthew gives Buoy's lovely ears a scratch as she sniffs around his legs in that lovely way of hers, and he feels himself beginning to calm down. He doesn't shut the front door, because Amy for some reason has not come into the house yet, and Gemma is loitering around the door-frame, committing to neither inside nor outside. He doesn't pay much attention to her nervous peregrinations – he's still annoyed at her. From the kitchen, he can hear Mum rumbling about, consolidating the dinner ingredients. Next, there's the metallic rattle as she fishes the garage keys from the bowl in the utility room. Anna, having extricated her big feet from her high heels and abandoned the shoes on the hall rug, swings her bedroom door open and deflates her body onto the bed.

MATTHEW

All of these things are normal, relative to their family. So normal that Matthew is in the process of jettisoning this accumulation of inanity from his short-term memory when his mum's voice rings out from the garage and down the hallway, in a tone he knows well – not angry, but with the precursor to anger primed within it: it is a voice that might become any number of things, depending on what happens next.

'Uh, folks? Did someone move the chicken?'

Matthew feels a fleeting relief, because he knows he knows fuck all about the chicken, and his genuine ignorance means he doesn't have to try and craft a strategic response. But also, why would anyone have moved the chicken? Then his mum is in the kitchen doorway, shortening the length of the hallway with the intensity of her look, summoning them into her gaze. Before anyone can say anything, though, Buoy, no longer being attended to by Matthew, scuttles into Anna's room. And then Mum is saying, 'Right, folks, someone speak up,' at the same moment that Anna, not visible but audible within her bedroom, is saying, 'Oh shit, Buoy, stop—' Gemma, meanwhile, is saying nothing, is biting her lip frantically. Matthew is glancing between the compass points of the moment, genuinely curious, when Buoy, emerging from Anna's bedroom with what looks like half a raw chicken in her furry mouth, scampers out the open front door with her prize, all too aware that what she's snuffled out from Anna's room is forbidden, isn't intended for her. And then Buoy has disappeared, beyond the frame of the front door, and now Anna is in the hall, barefoot and looking at Gemma with a guilty grimace. Gemma's face is the pale grey of the sea in winter, while Mum's expression seems to have altered the very composition of her face, because in the shadows of the hall Matthew almost doesn't recognise her, and as he glances from his family to the open front door and back again he wants to laugh, because all of this is funny, surely? It's funny that the chicken was in Anna's room – why was it in Anna's room? – and it's funny that Buoy has found it. But when he looks for longer at the various faces in the hall, it becomes clear that funny is not the shared consensus of the group, even though he can now hear Amy giggling outside, saying, in a bemused tone, 'What's that you've got there, Boo?' Even with this, funny is not the consensus, because Gemma looks like she's on the cusp of fainting, but why is she so distraught? He follows her haunted eyes, which dart between Anna – whose frown into the middle-distance is that of a person who has realised they have neglected some vital, primordial duty – and their mum, who is making her way, with threatening slowness, with grand, funereal steps, down the hall towards them. Funny is not the consensus, for some reason: the women around him are, to various degrees, anxious, rueful and furious, and the final thing Matthew notices in this methodical stock take of the confusing tableau is the sudden commencement of the fridge's loud and high-pitched chirp, emanating from the garage. Its plea that its door has been left open, and can someone please rescue its contents from the devastating effects of the world's atmosphere.

A moment later, Matthew is told to get out.
'Matthew, can you get out. Please.'
He's slow to understand. His mum is quick to repeat herself.
'Matthew, go. Get out. Shut the door.'

Buoy is sprawled contentedly on the sun-drenched tarmac, working delicately on the half-chicken. Amy is smoking a cigarette and watching the display.
'What's happening in there?' she asks. He shrugs, not wanting to admit how confused he is, how badly he wants her to explain to him what's happening. She laughs, and he wants to slap the cigarette from her hand. It must be so funny for her, that he doesn't

understand. Must be fucking hilarious, how ignorant he is. He scowls. He drops to his haunches and pets Buoy. Initially, the only sounds are the wind and the little dog's gentle, wet mastication. Then the wind dies, and he hears the low-pitched hum of irate disharmony, emanating from the walls and windows of the house. He listens to his mum call Anna selfish, Gemma incompetent. She lists the ways in which they are bad and wrong and deficient. He sighs, and peers up at his aunt.

'Can you go in and sort it?'

Amy squints towards the sea.

'Not sure I'm the right person to defuse tensions at the moment, Matt.'

He feels the frustration compacting in his torso, the steady upbuilding of anger through his body. What good are you, he wants to say. What good are you with your pretensions and your poetry and your weighty wisdom? What good are you if you won't do anything? Why aren't you doing anything, you stupid bitch?

The noises and insults continue – the low, unwavering pitch newly accompanied by a higher countermelody as Anna fights back. Matthew sighs again. He continues to stroke Buoy's ears, reminding himself to breathe. He twists on his ankles and

MATTHEW

looks at Amy more pointedly. 'Please, can you go in?' He hates that she's making him ask again, that she's making him treat her like some interventionist deity that can fix everything. The wind picks up again and briefly drowns out the chorus of anger. Amy drops her cigarette and grinds it into the tarmac with her heel.

'Okay. I'll go in.' She might as well be wearing a cape, he thinks, for how much she relishes being the saviour.

'Whatever,' he says. 'I'm going to take Buoy to the beach.'

She bends and puts her hand on his shoulder. 'It'll all be all right,' she says. 'It's been a tough day. Everyone just needs to get it out of their system.' She kisses her fingertips and presses them to the top of his head and walks towards the front door, rubbing at her chest as she does, as though massaging the funeral from her body. He feels bad at thinking unkind things about her – she's not a bad sort. At least she's trying to fix things. Maybe with her here, the evening won't fester. He tries to smile after her, eyes closed against the melting light. His mum is not quite shouting – she rarely actually shouts – but her enraged speaking voice is too loud, so loud that when you're exposed to it directly, it drowns out your thoughts, ensures you can't go anywhere in your own mind to avoid it.

Even with the barricade of the house's wall, it's too much. Amy opens the door, and there's a pause in the cacophony, and then the door closes, and he is alone. He stands, brushes the crumbs of asphalt off his knees, then gives Buoy's collar a gentle tug. 'C'mon, Buoy, let's go to the beach.' She rises, the chicken carcass secured safely in her mouth. They trot towards the steps.

Buoy takes the descent with a balletic grace, defying her age and hairy torso, defying the large item clamped in her teeth. Matthew darts behind her, failing to keep up. They take the hill in seconds, leaving behind the bottled mutiny. At the bottom of the steps she pauses to wait for him, tail beckoning, but just as he is about to reach her, she scurries forward. Past the barren holiday cottages. Out into the road.

'Buoy!'

He yells, then regrets it, because the tiny dog stops and turns to look at him before reaching the other side. A car rounds the bend at speed, and he throws his hands to his mouth, as though he could somehow take back the word which has already dispersed in the air. He watches with wide eyes as the blue Honda judders along the tarmac, straining to stop. It does, just shy of the furry body that is still twisted on the spot, Buoy's enquiring eyes focussed on Matthew and not on the mass of metal that almost rendered her and the chicken into fretwork on the road's surface. Aware, once more, of the brimming ewers of water and snot in his sinuses, he holds his breath to stop himself sobbing at the sight of his lovely and guileless dog, too attentive to Matthew's voice to consider her own frailty. He jogs out into the road, not looking at anything but her. Then: a protracted honk, detonating in his skull. He puts his hands to his ears and seizes up, trapped in the sound. When the echo in his head finally wanes, he looks up in the other direction, to see another car, bigger than the Honda, inches from his body. Behind the windshield of the huge, black 4x4, a man with a bald head is gesticulating furiously, and when Matthew looks back to Buoy, he can see the driver of the Honda, shaking his head in incredulity. The driver rolls down his window and raises his hands with a 'What the fuck?', but Matthew can't hear anything over the thumping of his own blood. He ducks his head and blinks through the film of tears, then strides forward to where Buoy is still waiting, happily, in the middle of the road. He gives her collar another tug, and they set off again. Once they are in the car park, he allows himself to look back. The drivers remain in the road, conspiring with each other, staring at him with disgust. He tries to mouth,

'Sorry,' but his muscles seem incapable of forming the syllables. He stumbles across the car park.

When Buoy is safely scattered to the sand with her prize, he allows himself to release his diaphragm and exhale, deeply. The tears roll despite themselves, his nostrils wet and claggy when he pulls his forearm across them. At the top of the dunes, he curls his spine, folding like a deckchair. He becomes aware of his joints and muscles – he applies pressure to different parts, straightening his knees to stretch the taut strings of his plantaris muscles; he lifts his head and feels the trellis of his spine hum with lazy protest. His body is his, and when he returns slowly to an upright position, he feels the bastard misery start to drain from his face. He breathes in the thick salt on the air and rolls his shoulders back. He watches Buoy trot leisurely along the dunes, navigating the desire lines carved among crops of vetiver. On the beach, she drops the chicken for a second and brings her hind leg to her ear, scratches idly. Now that she is far from home with her bounty intact, she conducts herself with a leisurely sense of victory. She takes the chicken back into her jaws and wanders. He watches her without expectation, and even when she is in the orbit of the wrecked piece of boat, he doesn't understand. Soon, she is at its opening, and a second later all Matthew can see is her floppy hook of a tail, waggling as she heads into the shipwreck's depths.

'Buoy!' he calls, sliding down the shifting levels in pursuit, sand crashing up and over the rigid backs of his school shoes, filling the pockets of air around his socks and burying his feet deeper in the stiff leather. He crashes forward and towards the wreck, but when he gets close, he halts, shuddering like the blue Honda. Buoy is out of sight, hidden somewhere in the depths of the shattered ship, and Matthew is stuck fast in the sand, incapable of getting closer to where she's gone, to where the light dies. He calls plaintively for her, desperate for her to scamper out, but she ignores him, choosing to remain an indeterminate part of the black mass. He imagines the woman's pale and expressionless face in the dark with Buoy, and he can't bear it: he falls heavily to the sand and rests his forehead on his knees. The only sound is his uneven, heavy breathing, caught in the chamber formed by his own collapsed body. Curled like this, his exhalations sound like the sea, hushing the world.

He's not sure how much time passes before he hears someone approaching, grunting and officious. Then Anna's voice says, 'Okay, Matt?' and she is at his side.

He looks up at her. She has a flush to her cheeks. He doesn't really know her at all. He wishes he did.

'Just you?' he says.

'Yeah.'

'Is it all sorted?'

She shrugs. 'God knows.'

Whatever has occurred in the house lingers on her – she casts innumerable spores into the air and the wind catches them, sending her extant energies across the beach. She looks haughty and indignant, but also something else he can't diagnose. He doesn't want her here, like this; he doesn't want to have to navigate the fallout of the catastrophe he was deemed too immature to understand. She puts her hand on his back, and he shrugs it off – he doesn't want her condescension, he just wants Buoy to come out of the wreck, to have not been destroyed by whatever might lurk inside it.

Anna sighs. 'It's all calmed down now, Matt. You know what it's like – it blows over as quickly as it starts up.'

It doesn't though, does it, he wants to say. It's all over her still. He says nothing.

'Where's the dog?' she asks.

'In there,' he says, gesturing to the wreck, and when she starts up with renewed vigour, 'For fuck's sake, Matt, why did you –' he just looks at her, then lowers his head back to his knees, willing her away, willing the wind to drown her out. It works – she stops talking. He inspects the tessellating fibres of his twill, synthetic trousers – black larvae packed tightly into cloth. In the humid tipi he has made of his body he continues to breathe, feeling the warm air condense. Anna calls to Buoy a few times, fruitlessly, then she says, 'I'll go get her.' A moment later, her voice takes on an ancient sonorousness, as her calls for Buoy reverberate off the wreck's walls. He waits, counting the ribbing in his grey socks, the eyelets in his shoes. He stays like this, placid and contained, until he hears her scream. A high-pitched, sharp-edged, staccato scream.

In an instant he is standing. He approaches. He goes on his tiptoes, as though darkness could be peered over like a wall. Nothing happens for a second, and then Anna is scurrying out of the wreck with Buoy in her arms, disgust drawing her features together. He says, 'What, what is it?' and Anna flings Buoy onto the sand and shakes her hair and wriggles her shoulders, covered with something invisible and invasive and crawling. He hates how whiny he sounds as he cajoles her – 'Seriously, what is it?' – but Anna has not concluded her dance, shaking her head at his incessance, shaking her head at whatever has lodged inside it. He feels that rigidity taking hold of him again, tries to control it in his voice, 'What is it, Anna?' She takes Buoy in her arms again and tells him to go and sit on the dunes, but he ignores her, because this is exactly the problem. This is the bullshit he's sick of: that he is always forced to loiter at a distance like a helpless child, while the adults mishandle the situation. He says, 'Fuck this,' under his breath, and strides towards the wreck. His frustration gathers like sediment in his joints and stiffens his movements, but he presses through; he protests against the sand and the wind and his body, and he makes it to the edge of the wreck. He takes his phone from his pocket and steadies himself. He allows the pathetic beam of the torch to guide him into the dark, too irritated to fear anything. Anna remains on the sand, watching him, and he's grateful for his anger — grateful for how it keeps him winched, how it stops him from turning and fleeing from the enclosing shadow.

Inside, everything stops. The blackness of the wreck devours both sound and sight. The smell of rot presses onto him from all sides, intensifying as he moves forward. After an eternity, the metal starts to taper to a point, and he is once more grateful for his anger, because an eternity, it transpires, isn't long enough to keep him from the furthermost end of the wreck. He is there, now, glancing around, scanning the edges with his torch. Finally, he arrives at something, and he takes a step back, then a step forward. He is now seeing what Anna saw, what Anna wanted to shake from her mind. What Anna wanted to keep from him. He breathes shakily. He translates what's in front of him. First, there they are: the small, meagre bones of the former chicken, licked clean by Buoy's tongue and punctured with crenels by Buoy's teeth. Then, next to them, are the larger bones. The bones that don't belong to the chicken. The longer, harder yellowed ribcage of a person. The long and slender bones of what was once a person.

The family sits on the beach in silence, settling into the last moments of the day. The early evening light is the colour scheme of a sliced grapefruit, and nobody is sure, now, how to behave. The wreck remains in its spot, looking to Matthew like it belongs there more now than it did before, like it has made itself comfortable. His mum takes her phone out of her handbag and unlocks it. They turn and watch her, expectantly. Nothing happens.

'I don't know who to call,' she says.

'The Guards?' Gemma says.

'Tout,' Anna mutters, issuing a derisive laugh.

'Grow up, Annie,' their mum says, though her heart doesn't seem to be in it.

'Seriously though,' Anna says. 'What the fuck are *they* going to do about it?'

'Ah sure,' Amy says. 'I'm sure they could take a few litres of seawater back to the station – detain it overnight.'

It's not that funny, but Gemma and Matthew laugh anyway, and their mum drifts off to make the call. Without her, the family gazes at the mephitic tableau before them, incapable of making language work. Eventually, Yvonne returns and says the Guards are going to send someone, but it'll be a while. Amy suggests a paddle – the salt water will be good for the weeping bubo on her big toe. She actually uses that word, 'bubo', and Matthew finds himself laughing again, because it's such an over-the-top and disgusting thing to say. His mum commences a mock scolding about the importance of appropriate footwear, and this takes them into a new moment, where something, seemingly, has been forgiven. Amy says something like, 'Shoes gratia shoe-is,' which Matthew doesn't understand, and then Anna says that

MATTHEW

Amy is a pain in the arse gratia-artis, which he also doesn't understand, but suddenly his mum is laughing uproariously, like it's the funniest thing in the world. With this, Matthew engineers a great swallow. It eases his entire body, and he's finally capable of digesting the day. He breathes deeply, and his mum reaches over and places her hand on the back of his neck and rubs it gently, like he's a dog or a child, and with this he feels a gratitude so immense he wants to laugh at the madness of it, so he does – he laughs, and it feels different to before, like it is the first true laugh he has ever issued into the world. It trickles softly into the currents of the evening. He gives his mum a hug, and she returns it, drawing him tightly and snugly into her body. It almost doesn't make sense, he thinks, how comforting it feels.

And he doesn't know this, but Yvonne is thinking about a day when Anna was much younger, when they went to London for the weekend. Matthew and Gemma, both still little, were left in the custody of Amy and Jess, so it was just the two of them, negotiating Trafalgar Square and Drury Lane. Anna allowed Yvonne to take her hand for road crossings, even though she was nearly thirteen, and when the sun came out, they took a table in front of an Italian café in Covent Garden. Anna had a prosciutto panini and a fancy lemonade, and they watched the tourists, jerking their heads like pigeons to take in the piazza. That evening they went to the theatre, and *The Sound of Music* was excellent, even though they got stuck with the understudy.

The next day, they went for a walk along the South Bank, Yvonne thinking they might have a quick spin around the Tate Modern before retrieving their luggage from the hotel and heading to the airport. The day was ashy, and as they neared the Globe there was a woman folded over, on her knees, holding a cup in her upturned hands. Her face was buried in her forearms, her brown hair pulled into a tatty ball at the nape of her neck. People strolled past, none paying her any mind, and as they approached, Yvonne noticed Anna slowing down. She turned, and Anna was a few paces behind, rootling through her tiny backpack, which Yvonne knew didn't contain much more than a purse full of coppers and some lip gloss. She told Anna to come on, but Anna said she wanted to give something to the woman. Yvonne told her not to, to come on, but Anna continued her search, at a standstill now. Yvonne told her again not to give anything to the woman, and at this final reproach Anna looked at her. Her face was a fresco of bewilderment and enquiry, underpinned by deep, deep suspicion. This ignited something in Yvonne, and suddenly she was dragging Anna by the arm, using more force than was necessary, using more force than she wanted to, and Anna was asking repeatedly why Yvonne didn't want her to help the homeless woman. This was Anna – never able to let something go – but this was also Yvonne, equally incapable of letting things go, albeit in a different way. This was them, and then Yvonne was shouting. She was shouting, in public, at her eldest daughter – a pretty, red-faced, scowling teenager – and Yvonne could tell, even in the moment, that while her own anger would burn itself out, the way Anna was looking at her now would never go away entirely. This made her shout more, because she was furious, truly furious at how unjust this all was, at how badly she wanted to not be shouting at Anna in public. But she couldn't explain that, because how could she? How could she explain that your reactions aren't always your own. How could she explain that, had things only been a little different, so might she have been.

 She'll give Sasha a call tomorrow, thank her for putting together such a good funeral. *Good* funeral? Nice funeral. Tasteful. Maybe she'll suggest a coffee. Maybe she ought to, for his sake. For her children's sake.

All she's ever wanted is to keep them safe, but at certain points, even that got corrupted. She looks at the black eternity contained within the shipwreck. Why did she ever think she could keep the darkness at bay? She thought some truths could be managed, that some truths *needed* management, that there were things to be shared and things to be suppressed. How can she be angry then, at Anna, or Gemma – how can she be angry at Amy, even – for thinking the same thing? Whatever Amy has done, it doesn't matter, because they've all made the same error, to different degrees. They all thought they could outmanoeuvre life, outmanoeuvre history.

And Matthew doesn't know this, but Amy is thinking about her new poetry collection, about the cancer that's finding its way into her cadences. She doesn't want to rely on disease for pathos – the loneliness of the human species should be more than adequate. Cancer is not an allegory for anything, just as death isn't. Death is just death, cancer just cancer. Moments dribble past, and to live is simply to attribute to each of those moments a weight determined by nothing more than your own inescapable singularity.

When she left Ithaca, the last thing she told him was to accept Sasha's invitation, and though she only

MATTHEW

saw them together a handful of times following their return, it was clear that Sasha loved him. She hopes he felt it in its fullness for as long as he could, just as she feels it now, the quiet exchange of care among limited bodies.

She's thinking about how best to tell them all. No doubt Yvonne will want to move in with her while she has treatment, will want to micromanage *every* step. How will that work, though, with the kiddies? The kiddies have just lost their dad, they shouldn't have to witness an atrophying aunt on top of that. Or maybe Yvonne won't want to do anything – maybe what has now been half-revealed will be sufficient to keep her at a distance. Maybe Amy should climb into the shipwreck and eat whatever that rotted monochrome primordia is. Maybe she should just duck out, now, gracefully. It might be less painful.

And he doesn't know this, but Anna is thinking about the stupid joke she just made, about how forcefully her mother laughed, and yet how equally forceful her mother's anger was, just before. She's thinking about how exhausting it all is, the hatred and the love – how sickening it is, the pride she feels at having made her mother laugh. Her mother will apologise shortly, Anna knows that, and as always this apology will be expected to lift an impossible load, will be expected to eradicate all the marks of injustice and overreaction and ad hominem savagery, and as always Anna will pretend that it has succeeded. No matter how warped she thinks her mother's view of things, Anna still wants to satisfy the impossible standards, to prove herself the winner of a rigged game.

It reminds her of a joke she made to her dad when she last saw him. It was stupid, appallingly so – a stupid pun about Philip Roth's prostate. He didn't need to laugh, but he did. He hissed through his teeth and clutched his abdomen. Another time, she made a similar, equally stupid joke to Alex, and he laughed so hard he had to regurgitate lager into his glass. This is all she ever wants, really – to hear the warmth and admiration in the laughter of someone she loves, when she tells a joke they find really, genuinely funny. It's all worth it – the agonising unpredictability, the anger, the grief, when she gets to feel that warmth. She misses her dad. She misses Alex. She can't wait to get back to him, away from this fetid wreck and Rob and the bones and her sordid transgressions. She measures her life in clean slates. Once she's back in London, she can throw this latest ruined one away.

* * *

MATTHEW

And he doesn't know this, but Gemma is looking but not seeing. She's thinking about the fur-lined hoodie, curled in its clean bundle on the chair in her bedroom. She'll return it to Christina, who won't ask questions. Gemma knows she should probably want to be at home, spending time with her family, but really, she just wants to be with her friends. She wants to be at Holly's house, yelling over a manic game of Twister or watching Netflix. She wants to send Ian a proper message, to ask him how study leave is going, to tell him about the bones in the wreck, or the glasses she found on the sea-floor – anything to make herself feel normal. At some point in the last year, she became horrified by her body, by how it seems to change on a daily basis. She almost didn't recognise herself, when she stripped down to her new bra and pants on Friday night. She looked at her body and it felt like something had gone wrong. That's why she wore the hoodie into the water.

She doesn't want to feel this way. She wants to be naked with another person, discovering pleasure without caveats, without these awful, intrusive thoughts.

Her phone vibrates in her pocket, rousing her. She brings it out and frowns at the message on the screen. It's from Ian: Hey. I **hope today went okay x** She stares at it till she's sure it's really there, then she slips the phone away again. She refocusses her eyes at the metal beast on the beach, at its frightening insides and its gangrenous seams. She feels an urge to crawl inside it and sit for a while, unseen. To be like the bones: quiet and alone and forgotten. Some days she feels like the shipwreck, like a blight on the landscape she moves through, an obstacle to every life form existing around her. She wonders if her dad ever felt like that.

And she doesn't know this now, but at some point, she'll learn just how little of what we try to conceal can remain undisturbed forever. Wanting dominion over anything only leads to misery, and the urgent search for meaning is, ultimately, a fleeting one. Nothing lasts, and nothing is ever really our own.

For now, though, she adjusts her hair. The family rises as one, and she tugs her top firmly down over her hips. Yvonne asks if she's okay, and she nods. They extend their arms at various altitudes, preserving balance as they head for the shore. Their fingers clamp at salinised atmosphere, closing over nothing. Eventually, they reach the sea, forming a snug huddle at the tide's edge like penguins. They waddle into the surf – hostile to this place and made of it. Five sets of feet find balance on the shifting sands. Behind them, the shipwreck stays where it is, open and broken.

NOTES

The quote on page 195 belongs to political theorist Jane Bennett and can be found in her book *Vibrant Matter: An Ecology of Things*, published by Duke University Press in 2009.

The quote on page 211 belongs to Seamus Heaney, from the poem 'Two Lorries'.

The quote on page 240 belongs to W.S. Merwin, from the poem 'The Shipwreck'.

ACKNOWLEDGEMENTS

Thank you to Emma Herdman and Gurdip Ahluwalia, the most dynamic and thorough and supportive editorial pairing I could ask for. Thank you to Elisabeth Denison, Ben McCluskey, Beth Farrell and the entire Bloomsbury team.

Thank you to my agent, Sophie Scard, with whom I have now been signed for eight whole years. What a time we've had. What rampant frivolities.

Thank you to the lovely, generous people who read this novel at various stages, or offered support as I tangoed with the colossal pigman of publishing: Dane Holt, Tara McEvoy, Manuela Moser, Michael Magee, Ali Lewis, Keiran Goddard.

Thank you to my mum, dad and brother for their love and ceaseless encouragement. Thank you to my incredibly talented friends, who make me a better writer by association, and who continue to enable me.

Thank you to Joey Connolly, the love of my life, without whom this book would not have been written – partly because a thousand conversations found their way into it in some shape or form, but also because nobody else would have the patience to ignore my repeated threats to quit.

A NOTE ON THE AUTHOR

Susannah Dickey is a writer from Derry. She is the author of two novels, *Tennis Lessons* (2020) and *Common Decency* (2022). Her debut poetry collection, *ISDAL*, was a *Guardian* and *Irish Times* Book of the Year, was shortlisted for the Forward Prize for Best First Collection, and won the inaugural PEN Heaney Prize and the Michael Murphy Memorial Prize. She lives in Belfast.

A NOTE ON THE TYPE

The text of this book is set in Fournier. Fournier is derived from the *romain du roi*, which was created towards the end of the seventeenth century from designs made by a committee of the Académie of Sciences for the exclusive use of the Imprimerie Royale. The original Fournier types were cut by the famous Paris founder Pierre Simon Fournier in about 1742. These types were some of the most influential designs of the eight and are counted among the earliest examples of the 'transitional' style of typeface. This Monotype version dates from 1924. Fournier is a light, clear face whose distinctive features are capital letters that are quite tall and bold in relation to the lower-case letters, and *decorative italics, which show the influence of the calligraphy of Fournier's time.*